EMPIRE OF THE GODS

IS THE TRUTH STRANGER THAN FICTION?

RAJENDRA KHER

Translated from the original Marathi by
PALLAVII ANTARKAR-JABADDE

CELESTIAL
BOOKS

ISBN 978-93-52015-55-9
© Rajendra Kher 2016
Translated and expanded from *Devanchya Rajyat*, in Marathi

Primary Translation: Pallavii Antarkar-Jabadde
Primary Editing: Sunita Kripalani
Cover: Fravashi Aga
Layouts: Chandravadan Shiroorkar, Leadstart Design
Printing: Thompson Press

First Published in English in India 2016 by
CELESTIAL BOOKS
An imprint of LEADSTART PUBLISHING PVT LTD
Unit 25/26, Building A/1
Near Wadala RTO, Wadala (East), Mumbai 400037, INDIA
T + 91 22 24046887 + 91 96 99933000 F +91 22 40700800
E info@leadstartcorp.com W www.leadstartcorp.com

To my wife, Seemantini,
to whom I owe my success as an author.

ABOUT THE AUTHOR

RAJENDRA KHER (b. 1961), a graduate of Pune University, has been writing for over two decades. He has published ten books in Marathi, all of which have been received with critical acclaim. Some of his bestselling novels have been translated into other languages. He has been honoured with five literary awards.

Rajendra has worked as an Assistant Director in the film industry, on documentaries, and as a Programme Director for a TV channel. Early in his career, he produced and directed the short experimental film, *Charlie Chaplin in India*. He has had extensive experience with writing scripts and screenplays. He has contributed numerous articles and short stories to newspapers and magazines. He can be reached at: rkher1961@gmail.com

OTHER BOOKS BY RAJENDRA KHER

Digvijay
Deha Zala Chandanacha
Geetambari
Dhananjay
Bindusarovar
Devanchya Rajyaat
Hollywoodche Vinodveer
Udayan
Dainandin Bhagavad-Gita (co-authored with Seemantini Kher)

CONTENTS

INTRODUCTION

The cosmos is colossal, yet minuscule.

Neither can the human intellect gauge its fullest extent, nor can the psyche encompass its minisculity completely. The 'intelligent' human being keeps swinging between these two extremes. As Lord Sri Krishna enunciates in the *Bhagavad-Gita*: 'Out of a thousand beings, just a single being endeavours to perceive my true essence; and only one in those thousands truly understands me in essence', meaning that only a rare person understands the Creator of all beings in essence, and yet, not totally.

It is said that even the famous scientist, Albert Einstein, utilised just about 13 percent of his brain. What can then be expected of the common man? Trying to know the expanse of the universe and its Creator is an impossible task. Man has still to explore 97 percent of the oceans present on Earth. Similar is the case with his brain and intellect. He has nebulous knowledge of perhaps 3 percent of the universe. His internal bodily functions too, are beyond his control. Innumerable questions remain unanswered, even today, such as why blood is red despite the consumption of other coloured foods? How does hydrochloric acid, which can actually burn the skin, form in our intestines, yet do us no harm? How are our glucose and blood pressure levels pre-determined? Who is the architect of all this? The unanswered questions are endless...

There is extensive, serious discourse in our ancient Indian scriptures such as the *Vedas*, *Puranas*, *Yogavashishtha* and *Bhagavad-Gita*, about the creation of the world, heaven, hell, earth and salvation. In framing the Vedic *suktas*, the sages mentioned several unfathomable incidents. Saints have, historically, through their teachings, preached good conduct to society, citing miraculous acts. They revealed that salvation, the ultimate truth or goal of human birth, is attainable in four ways:

Karma Marga – the path of right action

Yoga Marga – the path of psychic control

Bhakti Marga –the path of devotion

Jnana Marga – the path of knowledge (rational inquiry)

The Almighty is the ultimate truth man must strive towards. Yet, all of us are astounded by aspects such as *Para Brahma* (Supreme Power), *Saguna* (embodied manifestation/universal spirit, essence), *Nirguna* (His existence beyond omnipresent nature). The inspiration behind the creation of 84 lakh species on Earth, and Man himself, lies beyond the grasp of our intellect. It provokes us to muse on whether human beings are *Deva* (God's) creations, or those of the Supreme Power? Some sages may have understood the truth but deliberately refrained from writing it down, as a society engrossed in the material world is incapable of understanding it. An attempt to put forth the probable truth through the book *The Da Vinci Code*, created a public uproar.

Physicists have explored many unfathomable incidents/facts about the universe. Most discoveries reflect the concept of *tatvamasi* – the 'I Am That' principle. Despite being unable to decipher how millions of planets float over the gravitational pull, physicists have discovered numerous other concepts – such as the characteristics of planets in the solar system, black holes, galaxies, time relativity, the birth and death of stars, comets, etc. These facts, presented by eminent scientists, ought to be accepted as the principles of physics are undisputable, requiring proof. But the scientific approach towards nature and its Creator is restricted. Scientists are only now gaining a clearer idea of our solar system after having studied it for 200-300 years. The pace of scientific research and discovery is often influenced by political situations, international affairs, wars, etc. Thus it is difficult to explore Mother Nature, and thereby her Creator, with the help of science alone.

Whereas, in spirituality and philosophy, experience, faith and trust are major factors. When whole communities embrace these virtues, it helps to develop and maintain a high level of morality and good conduct among people. However, it can also lead to the practice of mere rituals instead of striving towards the Ultimate. Man has a reluctant attitude towards spirituality. He is disinclined to acquire answers about God's existence and His creations. It is mentioned in the *Bhagavad-Gita* that the major hindrance to achieving salvation is a lack of affection towards the Almighty. Man is uninterested in realising the true nature of the Almighty, which is the ultimate goal of life.

In *Empire of the Gods*, an honest effort has been made not only to explore God and the attainment of salvation, but also the fine association between science and spirituality. It explores the path to happiness by pinpointing the thoughts which arose from prolonged contemplation, in a kind of *prashnopanishad* (questionnaire). Sages have raised queries and answered them in the *Kenopanishad* but this book endeavours to find answers to unanswerable queries, using available proof. Utlimately it is for the reader to find personal answers, using judgement, logic and existing proof.

While modern society suffers the ills of destitution, depression and aimless living, some people have found peace and solace through introspection. I have attempted to unite these two extremes. I am no scholar but I have tried to decipher a path to desired human happiness. It is for the reader to absorb what appeals and set aside what does not. This book is not intended to hurt anyone's faith or spirituality. Rather, it is an attempt to attain ultimate happiness by going beyond religion, caste, creed, nationality, etc. It does not criticise any deity, but is a step towards knowing more about historic deities that have been worshipped till now as Gods, and to gain greater knowledge about them. As Lord Sri Krishna says in the *Bhagavad-Gita*: 'I am not achievable merely through rituals or by being religious'. This book has been written with the same rational approach.

PROLOGUE:
GODS AND THE SUPREME POWER

'Gods' and the 'Supreme Power' – are these words similar or distinct? They definitely require explanation. Modern astronomers, scientists, archaeologists, thinkers and students often assert that Gods were extra-terrestrials or aliens, and offer proofs thereto. These proofs seem quite convincing when judged logically and rationally, and viewed without prejudice. However, the idea that Gods were extra-terrestrial supernatural beings becomes hard to believe in the face of other factors such as religious beliefs, conventional social patterns, devotional ways, faith etc. Thus, the conventional mind rarely attempts to explore this outlandish path. It is content to remain within its comfort zone.

However, we do need to ponder over this topic in a rational spirit since the universe is undoubtedly governed by a supernatural, queer and cosmic energy. This lesser-known path is attainable by being impartial and sensitive, and can lead to the betterment of the human race. Many philosophers are engaged towards this end.

Following the study and contemplation on several scriptures and theoretical books on Gods, it can be stated that Gods and the Supreme Power (*Para Brahma*), are two distinct concepts. But this does not hold true from the viewpoint of philosophy and spirituality, which clearly state that the Ultimate Power resides everywhere, in every living thing. Therefore, God and the Supreme Power can never be different.

However, in defiance of this thought, God is still being analysed, even today, differently as Krishna, Rama, Shiva, etc.

Thus, considering God and the Supreme Power as two different concepts should not matter. But before that, a question about Man's Creator arises. If we assume the Supreme Power is the Creator, then the question arises as to why the Eternal Power should create such an 'imperfect' and 'helpless' creature such as the human? It might perhaps be justified from a philosophical point of view that human imperfections require them to connect with each other in order to function. They only merge with the Ultimate Power at the end of life's journey. Instead, what would it be like if we were to assume that human creation was the work of the *Devas*, experiments of the Gods, their hybrid generation? Whatever be the source, Man is an imperfect creation.

The two aspects, *Devas* (Gods) and *Para Brahma* (Supreme Power), are discussed in following chapters on the basis of logical reasoning and a fair bit of evidence. This book attempts to give the reader a tour of the universe, prompting intellectual introspection. It also intends to make vague concepts crystal clear. Being neither atheist nor devout, I have presented my writing from an unbiased point of view. My work does not intend to prove scientists to be less worthwhile, nor assert the excellence of the spiritual path.

Words have their own boundaries and cannot fully express emotions or meanings. At most they help to give expression to glimpses of this benighted world. Thus, the reader is directed to have his own outlook on the world. One has to traverse the unenlightened world oneself to experience divinity.

However, it is fundamental to clear all preconceived notions held to date. Misconceptions must be erased. Thoughts must follow a definite direction. Hence, we will traverse 'God's Kingdom' before entering into the 'Empire of the Supreme Power'. Unlike other trips when we carry baggage, here, we travel light, without a doubtful mind. Just travel with yourself. We are entering God's Kingdom.

PART I
WERE THE DEVAS ALIENS?

1. ADVENT OF THE GODS

The word *Dev* (God), has great implications. Derived from the Sanskrit *div,* it means 'to light up'. Its presupposed meaning is 'incomparable' and 'unique'. There are other meanings of *Dev,* which have been explained in the latter half of this book. 'A category that bears a divine body', is yet another. Several pilgrims say they have been witness to glorious *Apsaras* (courtesans) and *Devas,* descending in divine form to take a dip in Maan Lake in the latter half of the night. This supports the theory that they had divine bodies. However, since this is incomprehensible in normal human experience, one is left with either personal belief or disbelief.

The ancient Sanskrit grammarian, Yaskacharya, in his book, *Nirukta* (meaning 'derivation'), writes: *Deva:; Daanaat Wa Deepanaat Wa Dyotnaat Wa l dyusthano Bhavati Iti Wa l Yo Deva:; Sa Devata (Nirukta: 7/15).* This implies that the word *Dev* is formed from the Sanskrit verb roots *Da, Deep* or *Dyut,* which carry the connotation of giving alms, shining, or giving out light. He further says that *Devas* reside in *Dyu-loka,* that they are high-ranking, chaste souls who experience a highly elevated and heavenly life. Those who posses matter plus power, accompanied by additional values, are *Devas.* According to another erudite commentator, Sayanacharya, Devas implies 'giving of light' or 'glowing'.

Exactly where is this *Dyu-loka* situated? From where do these Gods or *Devas* come to earth, shining and emitting light? Certainly not on Earth, so is it somewhere in outer space? The Sanskrit word *Loka* means 'planet'. Which then was the planet they may have come from?

There wasn't just one God, but many. One finds references to this in mythology and ancient scriptures like the *Vedas*. There are also many vehicles associated with the Gods. Let us look at some of the names of vehicles used by Indian deities – Garuda (the mythical bird of Lord Vishnu), Airavat (the elephant of Lord Indra), the tiger of Goddess Kali, the mouse of Lord Ganesh, etc. Were these vehicles symbolic or perhaps metaphors? Or were they aircraft of varied shapes?

There is a recent trend in the West to shape cars like various animals. Gods' aircrafts could perhaps have been the outcome of similar ideas. There are numerous stories in the *Vedas*, *Puranas*, and etched on pyramids in symbolic language, of *Devas* travelling in aircraft. The vehicles they drove had variety. The Gods fought battles in them and sometimes lost and died as well. Therefore, the literal meaning of the word *Div*, which means 'to shine', reflects a different meaning.

Were the pilots who manoeuvred the shining, flying chariots through the sky called Gods? Were the Gods, in fact, highly advanced beings from outside our solar system? What was their purpose in being on Earth and living in the company of underdeveloped and uncivilized humans? Were the *Devas* thus the most advanced community on Earth? And were humans astounded by the advancement displayed by these Gods? Was Man awed by it all and, in that inspired state, dedicated his life to these mighty Gods? Did he place life's problems and personal disputes before them for resolution? Like the British, did the *Devas* employ the policy of 'divide and rule' in order to gain a hold over Earth, and towards this end, train heroes in the use of arms?

Was the lifestyle of the Gods different from that of the humans on Earth? Did they deliberately locate their abodes in remote areas for reasons of safety? Despite their advancement in physics, were they threatened by someone or something? Did they attempt to establish human culture on Earth? Was the definition of religion, 'that which forms and nurtures a society', introduced by them? Was the establishment of religion an experiment on an underdeveloped and uncultured human society?

There are innumerable questions of this nature which arise and all the answers are in the affirmative. There are many stories written in the *Rig Veda*, the *Mahabharata*, as well as myths about the advent of Gods, their inhabitance, their advancement in physics, and their aerial journeys, etc. These have been considered symbolic stories until now. While literature is loaded with symbolic content, can we assume all that was written to be merely symbolic?

In a scene from the movie, *The Gods Must Be Crazy*, a family lived in a remote and isolated part of the Kalahari Desert. They did not even know how to build a hut for themselves, let alone make their own clothing. They were oblivious of the advanced and well-developed city in South Africa, just 500 miles away. In fact, they were ignorant of the existence of other humans on Earth. At the sight of an airplane in the sky, they presumed it was the Gods traversing the heavens. One day, the pilot of an aircraft dropped an empty bottle from the sky. The bottle found its way to the family in the Kalahari Desert. It led them to believe the bottle was a gift from God. The head of the family kept pondering over the utility of the bottle and the intention of God in presenting it to them. This led them to discover different uses for the bottle, such as breaking roots, crushing leaves, curing snake's hide, etc. It did not stop there; they found they could create sounds by blowing through it as well. Each one now desired to have the bottle, and this led to bitter fighting. As per the decision of the head of the family, his son set off on the journey towards the end of the 'flat' Earth in order to return the divine bottle to the Gods. On his journey he confronted God. The story unfolds with amusing details.

Could the human race on Earth have experienced similar incidents 5,000 years ago? What must have taken place then? Imagine Gods landing their airplanes or vehicles on Earth. This advanced capability of the Gods in physics must have fascinated the humans of the time, who were completely ignorant of such things. The Gods' huge airplanes, the gold and illuminated stars embedded on them. All this must have left man in awe!

People might have been familiar with carts drawn by bullocks or donkeys, and for some people of rank, horses-drawn vehicles. To them, these flying chariots of the Gods must have seemed to be pulled by horses! Since the horses could not be seen, it meant they had invisible characteristics. The hearts of those early humans must have filled with gratitude after having practically met with God. They must have tried to emulate God, being impressed by His supreme form. They had faith that the Gods could transform their lives and they would then know the real meaning of existence. Subsequently, the Gods apparently returned to their own lands, having spent hundreds or thousands of years on Earth.

Astronauts carved into the rocks of Sego Canyon, Utah, USA, in 5000 BC, clearly show them wearing helmets with antennae.

The modern English word 'planet' had an alternative Sanskrit word – *loka*. The humans on Earth may have bemoaned the Gods' return to their own land and the Gods may have consoled them saying, 'Practise good conduct, the way we have conferred it upon you. Attain self-realisation. Practise humanity. If these things are in danger, we will return to revive them.' An entire generation that met the Gods in person must have narrated these events to their children, it being impossible for them to put it all in writing. Nor did they consider recording these events for posterity. Hence, they narrated an auditory form – *Shruti*, making it easy for the next generation to recite it. This recitation turned into memories over the next few generations – *Smruti*. In this way each generation assured the next, 'God is there; have faith'.

Later, the system the Gods had set up may have collapsed and the remaining virtuous ones may have resorted to prayers to the Gods. These prayers could have included stories of their forefathers. A monument may have been erected for the purpose of directing those prayers and the concept of a ringing bell included in addressing their complaints to Him.

We have discussed the facts relating to Gods, their chariots, and their descriptions mentioned in the Mahabharata. Is this a realistic rendition or does it all sound far-fetched? It definitely does not sound like fantasy. But if the Gods were truly extraterrestrial beings, how could this be proved?

2. FLYING CHARIOTS

'The bright chariot driven by Indra *sarathi* (charioteer) Matali came whirling around in the dark. It had a quaky impact like that of a giant thunder all over. It had several volatile objects making loud sounds like a clap of thunder, loud roars, clanging objects like swords, fearful batons, powerful sounds, blinding flashes of lightning [*Vidyutashcha, Mahabharata*: 43/4], thunderbolts, artillery which included cannonballs and guns [*vayusphotaha*]. The supernatural chariot was pulled by 10,000 super-powerful horses [*Mahabharata*: 43/7]. The onlookers remained dumbstruck at the sight of such an illusory divine chariot.'

This excerpt from the *Aranyak Parva* of the great Indian epic, *Mahabharata*, in which Maharshi Vyas intricately describes the giant chariot of Lord Indra, is surely a topic of contemplation. The fact that an object could fly through the atmosphere at enormous speed, making a thunderous sound, imparting a quivering impact, became known to the modern world only after the discovery of supersonic aircraft and jets. Then how was it known to more backward human beings 5,000 years ago? Possibly Sanskrit words like *ashani, astra, mahatejasvi, vidyullata* were alternative terms for missiles, weapons, etc. 'The chariot was driven by ten thousand horses', appears to be impractical, nonetheless, this metaphor is explicable of the way the huge chariot *Airavat*, Indra's spaceship, may have flown – with 10,000 horse power (HP), astounding viewers. It is interesting that the word *airavat* resembles 'air'.

Here, it is best to give due consideration to mythology and India's ancient literature. One finds a generous use of metaphors to explain incidents indirectly, through poems, parables or short stories. For example, Lord Indra putting Vrutrasur to death is depicted by the sunrise. Lord Laxman cutting off Shurpanakha's nose signifies he won the province ruled by Shurpanakha as Governor. Often, it becomes difficult to ascertain the exact meaning or truth from metaphors. Thus this may be true of the metaphor of Lord Indra's chariot being pulled by 10,000 horses as well. Such detailed descriptions in the *Mahabharata* are bewildering. Further chapter 161 mentions that Matali and Arjuna drove the chariot through the sky, describing it thus: 'Matali propelled his Indra-chariot in such an elegant manner that it was like a smokeless torch moving through the clouds'. What does the 'smokeless torch' in the dark of night remind us of in recent times? These aspects are categorically explained in the *Mahabharata*. In chapter 164, *shloka* 38, there is further clarification about Indra's chariot saying God Indra gets distracted at the time his chariot takes off. Matali says to Arjuna, "O Arjuna, it is very commendable that unlike God Indra, you seem so composed, seated in the chariot". Even today, air passengers fasten their seat belts for takeoff.

Chapter 164 describes Arjuna and Matali's encounter with *Nivaatkavach* demons. Despite the fact that the chariot was being drawn by 10,000 horses, it seemed to be pulled by fewer numbers and the chariot was easily steered by Matali. In modern thought, this *shloka* seems to compare the efficacy of the chariot to an engine of 10,000 HP.

Several similar examples about Gods and their chariots are cited in the *Mahabharata*, *Rig-Veda*, *Ramayana*, and in mythology as well. There is a mention in Bana's *Harsha-charita* that, the *Yavan* (Ionians), designed a flying device to carry the King. Similar mention is made of Mandhata, by Avanti Sundar of Dandi, who made use of a flying machine to travel to his son's abode. There is also a reference of a flying wooden cock in Somdevbhatta's *Katha Saritsagar*. A young lover, Vishlil, learned the art of making the flying machine from Yavan.

Meghdoot by Kalidasa is a legend that mentions aerial travel 15,000 years ago. Such a detailed description of Earth is impossible unless viewed from space. This means that in ancient times there were aircraft, and this fact should be accepted. Dr. David Childress, in his book *Vimana – the anti-gravity handbook*, explains ancient India's aeronautics well. According to him, the UFOs sighted on Earth long ago were considered to belong either to aliens or assumed to be army experiments. He is of the opinion that considerable thought should be given to ancient Indian aircraft though few people are of the opinion that ancient Indian satellites might still be present today.

Dr. Childress further states that King Ashoka formed an intelligence committee comprising nine scientists who wrote *gupta grantha* (secret books). King Ashoka maintained a high-level of secrecy about these ancient books, which had mystical descriptions. He feared they would be destroyed by evil-minded people. The book, *The Secrets of Gravitation*, is not known to anyone today, perhaps safely stored somewhere in Tibet. It is said that Chinese students found some ancient Sanskrit documents in Lhasa. According to the information in these documents, certain kinds of aircraft floated in the Earth's atmosphere, and even in space, using the principle of *laghima*, which in English means 'power of the ego'. These aircraft were also termed 'weapons'. Astronauts could go to any planet using the connected parts. Words like *antima* (cap of invisibility) and *garima* (to become heavy as a mountain of lead), have also been used in this Sanskrit manuscript.

These aircraft would operate on the principle of anti-gravity. There is also mention in Sanskrit literature that the aircraft could function underwater. Some say that Chinese scientists have applied this information in their space programme. One can find similar mention in *shlokas* in the *Rig-Veda* as well. There are references to aircraft in the *Ramayana* as well – two-tiered aircraft shaped like saucers. There is also mention of an aircraft with stairs, flying at great speed.

There is a science book in Sanskrit, *Samarangana Sutradhara*, written by King Bhoj in the 11th century; in chapter 31, there is information about air travel. In its 230 *shlokas* there are plenty of details on topics like aircraft assembly and takeoff, normal and forced landings, journeys of 1000 miles, and measures to be taken in case of birds crashing against the aircraft. These aircraft are believed to be have been able to travel within the sun's and the stars' orbits. It also includes information such as aircraft should be of lightweight material, able to ferry passengers, and operate noiselessly. The engine has specifications regarding safety measures in case of fire.

Similarly, there is information on various aircraft movements: 'These aircraft travel long distances, flying upwards, downwards, diagonally, and making loud trumpeting sounds. However, these sounds can be transformed into musical tones as and when required...' Is it true then that Indra's chariot (or spaceship), was used as a simile to describe Indra's elephant? How else can an elephant fly in space? *Samarangana Sutradhara* also tells us that such shining planes could be propelled to just about anywhere. The Gods riding in the planes thus had an aerial view of the activities on Earth and were able to intervene accordingly. Even so, does it tally with the scenes described in ancient literature, when Gods showered flowers from the heavens?

William Clarendon, a student of Indian studies, in his translation of *Samarangana Sutradhara*, has stated that aircraft the size of temples, could be built, with four mercury fuel containers which made the sound of roaring lions. This prompts another thought: Does the structure and shape of ancient temples, the sanctums and the deities within its narrowing peaks, substantiate the Gods' existence, or a prototype of the Gods' flying spaceships?

Aeronautics, a book written in the 4th century BC by the great sage, Bharadwaj, was found in a temple in 1875. Surprisingly, it referred to older books, which meant that Indians then were familiar with aeronautics thousands of years ago. The book contains material related to aircraft mechanism, steering, precautions to be taken during difficult take-offs, unfavourable weather conditions like thunder and lightning, and on how to convert the plane's fuel to solar energy at a crucial time. There are eight chapters and *Aeronautics* includes many precise diagrams as well. Three types of aircraft are well explained. The outer casing (fuselage) and the tools of these aircraft were fire-resistant and indestructible. The book contains information about 31 important parts in the aircrafts and 16 kinds of raw material required to manufacture the spare parts. A yellowish-white fuel, like gasoline, was used in the aircraft. Reference is made to 70 officers and 10 experts by sage Bharadwaj, and to combustion and pulse-jet as well. The aircraft would take off vertically, like helicopters.

The three aircraft – Rukma, Triputa and Shakuna, are studies in crude mechanical electrical technology, electromagnets, cranks, shafts, warm years, pistons, heating coils, electric motor turning and propellers. The Rukma aircraft had lifting fans that were powered by electric motors. It is mentioned that the pilot needed to know 32 secrets of the plane and these secrets are given as well. The *shloka* written by sage Bharadwaj says:

> About the Rukma Viman:
> *Peeth Rukmavimanasya kurmakaaram pakalpayet l*
> *Witasthihasaayaamam Gaatramekavitaastikam ll*
> About the Shakuna Viman:
> *Tathaiva Waatapaayantro Dikpradarshadhwajastayaa l*
> *Pashchaachhakunsyasntraascha Tatpakshadwayameva cha ll*
> *Vimaanotpekshanaartha Tatpucchabhaagastyayaiva hil*
> *Tato Vimaanasanchhrakaarannyoushmyakayantrakahall*

In short, scholars are of the opinion that the technical know-how and space technology prevalent in ancient times were of a far more advanced order than used in spaceships, rockets and related technology today. However, this knowledge no longer exits. Books like *Aeronautics* are now referred to only as proof it once existed.

Diagrams of an aeroplane, helicopter, glider and space shuttle, carved on the walls of the New Kingdom Temple, Abados, south of Cairo, 3000 years ago.

Hitler and the Nazis had special interest in ancient India and Tibet. Every year, a batch of Nazis would visit India and Tibet for research, from which they obtained scientific information related to aeronautics. The Nazis made use of pulse-jet engines in their V-8 Rocket Buzz Bombs.

Russian scientists came upon an ancient compass in the caves of Turkey and the Gobi desert. They found a drop of mercury was used in the compass, which was shaped like a glass cone. This instrument may have been used by astronomers as a guiding tool. Other references have not only been found in Mohenjo Daro sculptures but also in Easter Island, in Rongo Rongo script, and perfectly matches the one in Mohenjo Daro.

It can easily be proved that aeronautical science was familiar to the ancients in a much more advanced form than we know today. But how did our forefathers gain this knowledge so long ago? How could they have built advanced aircraft when the study of physics was not even in its primary stages? How then did nomadic people fight battles sitting in chariots that were so technologically advanced? Were the Gods playing a role, as it were? There could have been two different groups – one composed of ordinary people, and the other of advanced deities, who travelled in their chariots. Sage Naarad Muni was said to travel through space. There is mention in the *Ramayana* of the mighty King Ravana acquiring the Pushpak aircraft from the God Kuber. What was this aircraft like? Some scholars are of the opinion that the Pushpak was a huge, diamond-studded vehicle created by Vishwakarma. It had windows of pure gold. This aircraft was at Ravana's disposal in Lanka.

In the *Vedas*, planes like the *Agnihotra-Viman* and *Gaja-Viman* have been described. According to scholars, *Agnihotra-Viman* signifies an aircraft with two engines while the *Gaja-Viman* has a cluster of engines. References to research point out that these aircraft were of different shapes, sizes and functions.

Also, there is frequent mention of King Shalwa's aerial kingdom Icchaagami as well as Indra's chariot over the forest Khaandav, the presence of Gods and their chariots for a *Rajasuya Yagna* held by King Yudhishtra in the *Mahabharata*. King Shalwa of Icchaagami waged a war against Dwaraka. Lord Krishna had built an impregnable wall around Dwaraka, making it impossible for the enemy to enter by land. But King Shalwa attacked Dwaraka by air. He bombarded it with missiles. Krishna was not presentat the time. When he returned, he found Dwaraka devastated. Enraged by the destruction caused by Shalwa, he crossed several rivers, countries and mountains, and reached Shalwa's territory.There he learnt that Shalwa had gone on a visit to an ocean near Martikawat. Krishna's army advanced towards the ocean. He could see Shalwa's island floating. The battle began, with Shalwa resorting to tactics of deceit. Finally, Lord Krishna hurled a fire weapon towards Shalwa's floating island. The weapon hit the island so hard that it shattered into pieces that scattered all over the ocean. This detailed description of ancient events has been chronicled in the *Mahabharata* by sage Vyas.

Both foreign and Indian scientists have studied the ocean in the area mentioned and have successfully obtained proof, concluding that the Icchaagami kingdom of King Shalwa might have been a flying saucer. Apart from this, the *Mahabharata* includes many references to aircraft like the *Maya Sabha*, built by Mayasur, which was shaped like a modern-day aeroplane. There were also steps to climb into Indra's chariot and similarly, there were steps to enter Arjuna's famous chariot as well. These descriptions seemed symbolic till the time modern aeroplanes were invented. Considering the minute details mentioned by the sages, would it then be right to consider these details merely symbolic?

In recent times, a Mumbai student, Shivkar Bapuji Talpade, designed an aircraft based on Vedic techniques by studying ancient aeronautics. Talpade, a Sanskrit scholar, came across the *Bruhadvaimanik Shastra*, written by the sage Maharshi Bharadwaj, which inspired him to actually assemble an airplane. Along with Vedic literature, he also studied *Vimanchandrika* by the great spiritual ascetic, Narayan, *Vimanyantra* by the sage Shounak, *Yantrasankalpa* by Garga Muni, *Viman Bindu* by the spiritual guide, Vachaspati, and *Vimandnyanarka Prakashika* by the sage Dhundiraj. He then presented his first aeroplane – *Maruta-shakti*.

Maharaja Sayajirao Gaikwad of Baroda supported Talpade in his mission in every possible way. Talpade demonstrated his creation in 1895 at Mumbai's Chowpatty Beach, in the presence of the Hon. Judge Mahadev Govind Ranade, and other scholars. On 17th December 1903, the Wright Brothers flew the so-called first modern aircraft, at a height of 120 feet. But eight years prior to this, Shivkar Talpade had propelled his aircraft in the sky at a height of 1,500 feet, in the presence of scholars of aeronautics. Despite this, his work was never recognized and he was burdened with many restrictions imposed by the British East India Company. Talpade could not carry out further experiments due to a lack of funds and other impediments. Thus, the Wright Brothers are credited with the first takeoff and flight in an aeroplane in the modern world. Talpade died unsung in 1916. The first ever experiment in aerial flight, based on Vedic knowledge, went disregarded. The great knowledge imparted by the Gods somehow got stuck in bureaucratic routine. The Western world achieved greater success by carrying out new inventions based on the study of physics.

Some scholars reject the idea of ancient flying machines as mentioned in ancient Indian texts. They define *vimana* as 'measuring a specific area or land', relating to royal palaces and their intricate structures. They even state that the text *Vaimanik Shastra*, is totally false. It is not an ancient text and was found in 1918. The description in it of what must have sounded like a technical idea in 1918 or 1952, is that of a mercury-vortex engine. The *Vaimanik Shastra* (Science of Aeronautics), indicates that *vimanas* used a propulsion system based on a combination of gyroscopes, electricity and mercury, which is not possible. Mercury is an unusual element – a liquid metal which was also a good conductor of electricity. Hence it is useless as a fuel. They even disregard the Pushpak Viman of King Ravana.

The existence of aeroplanes in the ancient period can be disputed since the knowledge of scholars contesting the existence of the Pushpak aircraft and the science of aeronautics is restricted. Western historians believe the Vedic period to be from 500 to 1500 BC, but Indian scholars believe the Vedic period to be around 8,000 years B.C. Western historians ignore ancient knowledge, as seen through a modern perspective. Although their approach cannot be assessed at present, ancient times definitely witnessed a great advance in the science of aeronautics, mathematics and physics. Thousands of years ago, this knowledge may have been introduced by the Gods to the primitive humans who referred to them as the 'Supreme Power'.

3. GODS – EXTRATERRESTRIAL HUMANS?

Some years ago, the archaeologist, Erich Von Däniken, put forth the following theory: a thousand years ago, war broke out between two groups of superhumans, from two different planets. Because of this war, they considered it unsafe to inhabit their own planets and felt the need to explore other planets for their safety. One group discovered Earth to be a better place to dwell. Hence, the Gods, or advanced humans, made Earth their abode. In order to adapt to Earth's atmosphere, they used gas masks. They were pioneers in setting up the fundamental blocks of an advanced human race. They were the ones who formed a hybrid human race on Earth by connecting themselves with the existing barbarians. Nonetheless, they faced a threat from their enemies in the universe. In order to remain safe from these advanced enemies, who could easily locate them with their hi-tech aids, the Gods created underground dwellings where they could hide (excavations have unearthed remains in central Asia). Later, the Gods created huge pyramids for their use. They also set up space stations and transmitters on the fifth planet of the solar system. When their enemies landed on this fifth planet, they got trapped. The superhumans on Earth destroyed the fifth planet remotely. Bridging the distance of 30 crore miles between the fourth and fifth planets of today's solar system seems unfathomable to us.

The habitation of the Gods on Earth lasted for a few thousand years. The pyramids and other such momuments, when compared to modern constructions, render researchers speechless. Däniken opines that the pyramids of Egypt and Mexico are accomplishments of the Gods. There are also murals, attributed to the Godlike race, with humans depicted, found in various caves around the world. The humans on Earth were the Gods' creation and they came from another planet within the galaxy or somewhere near Sirius (*Vyaadh*) – *this was* the theory put forth by Däniken, who also denied the theory of genetics formulated by Darwin.

The Great Pyramid at Gaza, Egypt.

Erich Von Däniken's premise faced criticism all over the world. Confusion is inevitable when preconceived notions are shattered. He was accused of lying. Perhaps such consequences were the reason scholars have not publicised their knowledge of the ancient period to the world, preferring to retain social harmony rather than expose the truth as facts.

Similarly, researcher Zecharia Sitchin points out that the entire Nibiru civilisation which existed on a small planet, was wiped out. According to Sitchin, Nibiru was the twelfth planet of our solar system and revolved in a clock-wise direction. One year on Earth has 365 days, whereas the Nibiru year has 3600 days. The members of this group used to visit Earth. This was the warring community that would attack others in order to acquire gold. This is mentioned in Sumerian mythology. These beings were possibly of the reptilian breed. Anunaki, God of the Sumerians, is portrayed with a combination of reptilian and human qualities. It is believed by the descendants of this group, that humans were created from the DNA of reptiles.

The evolving front portion of the human brain is short and quite primitive, just like the full brain of reptiles. Hence, this part of the brain is known as Reptile Brain. In the primary section of the brain, several emotions like anger, fear, hatred, envy and satiety, emerge. After millions of years of evolution, other aspects such as practical experience, morality and control, made space for themselves. This reptilian part of our brain determines the eruption of anger, frustration and negative emotions – the beast in humans surface.

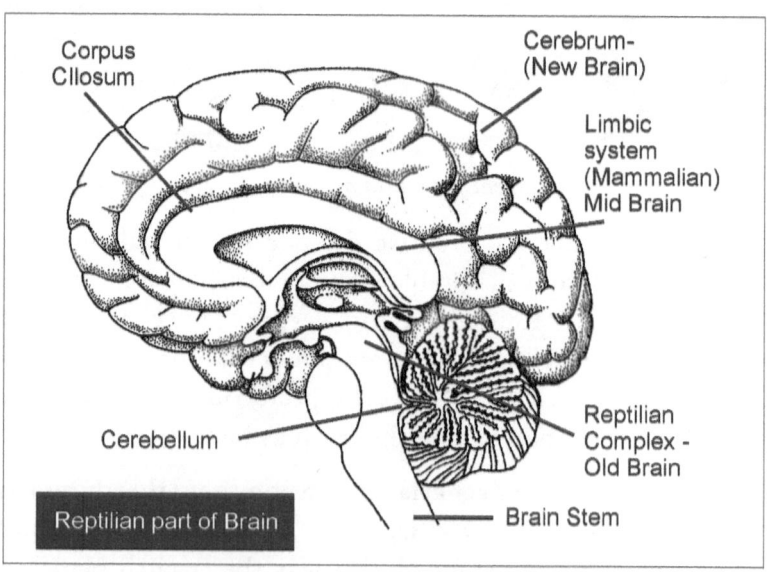

The reptilian part of the brain.

Ancient humans may have symbolised this aspect in the form of the Sumerian God. Does God Vishnu, seated on a cobra impart a similar message? Similar stories are found in the mythology of other countries as well. There is mention in primitive folk tales of extraterrestrial humans who came to Earth in search of gold, which they found underground and excavated it. Slaves were made to work in these mines. They created *humans* to work as slaves, carrying out research on the DNA of monkeys and themselves. Later, Enalil and Enki, the slaves, went against the Nibirus, the Gods. The Gods then caused a deluge and destroyed them.

In the Bible, the Hebrew word *Elohim* means 'God' or 'one who has come from outer space'. It is alleged in Genesis 1/26: 'And God said let us make man in our own image, after our likeness'. God says, 'Let us make man like *us*' and not 'like *me*', which clearly shows God was not one entity but a plural form. In the ancient period, the Sumerian civilisation was quite advanced. Suddenly, this civilisation became extinct, nobody knows why. But the astounding history of extraterrestrials is engraved on bricks in occult signs. There is an epic, *Gilgamesh*, of the Sumerian civilization, in which much has been written about chariots being propelling through space with huge emission of fire. Various stories in *Gilgamesh* resemble narrations in the *Old Testament*. The stories of Moses and also that of the deluge, have been noted in this epic, in different words. Similar to Eden of the *Old Testament*, there is a breathtaking narration of Dilmun in the *Epic of Enki and Ninhursag*.

That the *Devas* (Gods) were extraterrestrial superhumans has several proofs. Let us list some points of reference found in ancient books, irrespective of their accuracy.

1.   **Galaxy:** To the extreme end of our solar system is our galaxy *Aakash-Ganga*, the Milky Way. The mass of this galaxy is at least 1000 billion times that of the Sun. There

might be 400 billion stars, large and small, in this galaxy. Scientists Frank Drake and Carl Sagan have put forth theories related to life in the galaxy. Considering an average of their famous formulae, the number of intelligent and advanced civilisations in the galaxy goes up to a minimum of 10 lakh. Many of these advanced civilisations could be situated at a distance of 100 to 1000 light years away from Earth. This means that if a human travels by any airplane at the speed of light, he would require 100 to 1000 years to reach those planets in the galaxy where these advanced civilisations exist. Today, this seems incredible to the developed human being on Earth.

Yet, thousands of years ago, could the superhumans in the galaxy have, by their own wits, travelled this seemingly improbable distance? What measures might have been adopted? Probably, they were well-acquainted with the concept of black holes and made use of it to traverse immense distances.

2. **Speed terminology:** It is still not possible for us to travel through space at the speed of light since humans are unable to tolerate the speed and there are no means available to do so. But what if we could defy our body's limitations? What can move at lightning speed without being confined to the body's limitations? Swami Vivekananda once said that the speed of the mind was unimaginable. By riding on that capability, with perfect control, one can journey through the universe.

Using the terminology of physics, electro-magnetic waves move without restraint at unimaginable speed. Above all, they can be carried to any planet in the form of energy. It would be possible to create a living body if liquid was present there. Scientists are researching this concept but have not met with success.

While the mind and soul may be able to tour the universe, the body cannot accompany them. But what if a human could put down his food sheath, *annamaya kosh* – the outermost body, here on Earth, and then recreate it on another planet with the help of the air sheath, *praanamaya kosh – the second body or life force*, and *manomaya kosh* – the third body or the mind, the centre of human existence, and his intellect sheath, *vigyaanamaya kosh* – the fourth body? Then he could easily travel to distant planets at speeds greater than light. This is possible, according to the science of yoga, described in *Yoga Darshan* by Bhagwan Patanjali, thousands of years ago.

Assuming that the Gods arrived from one of the planets of the galaxy, can it be inferred that the relevant planet was at a distance of just 10 days, based on the calculations of the speed of *manomaya kosh*? Is this why the journey of the soul after death is believed to be of 10 days duration? Does this belief exist because humans have their roots in the galaxy?

Lord Sri Krishna points out in chapter 15 of the *Bhagavad-Gita*: *Urdhwamulamudhaha Shaakham Ashwatthampraahuravyayam* – the root of this world-tree is high and it has branched below. Considering its literal meaning, it is clear that one end is the Earth and at the other where humans have their origins. The roots of man have spread up from below.

Scholars are of the opinion that of the five elements of nature i.e. earth *(prithvi)*, water *(jal/aap)*, air *(vayu)*, fire *(tej/agni)* and ether *(akash)*, ether is the only one not within our reach but fills all of nature. It is high, meaning that the roots of the world-tree are in space. If this is considered to be true, then what of the fact that ether is also present in atoms and molecules of matter as well? What exactly does 'high' mean? Has man evolved from space?

3. **Speed:** When a man dies, prayers are said for his ongoing journey, but where is the journey from and to where? A journey towards another *yoni* or birth or towards a higher plane, is understandable. But why the need to journey somewhere far to attain another birth? Why is it required? Most people wish to be born in a higher class family in their next birth. When the soul leaves the body, why not travel for ten days on Earth? Advanced souls wish to go to Heaven. This again brings up the question: What and where is Heaven? Is it in this galaxy? Does the journey in a disembodied state from Earth to Heaven require a period of ten days? One query kindles another.

4. **A virtuous king's journey to *Swarg* (Heaven):** The *Mahabharata* by sage Vyas is considered to depict history by today's scholars. It was written with an unbiased approach by the great sage, and the epic reflects his great intellect. His descriptive style is so real that it leaves the reader spellbound. But there are several events in the *Mahabharata* which seem unreal and incoherent to a rational mind. Nonetheless, this does not deny they occurred.

If today's flourishing human civilisation was endangered after 200 years and then prospered 1500 years after the Stone Age, then all the books describing today's progress in physics and technology and things like remote controls, television sets, journeys to the moon, the internet, cell phones etc, would seem imaginary and highly improbable concepts to humans of that time.

Should we label the incidents of the *Mahabharata* which we feel to be beyond our intellect, as far-fetched and highly improbable, and so overlook them? Or should we consider them poetic and symbolic? Erich Von Däniken, in his book, *Chariots of Gods*, mentioned for the first time that our past is much more shocking than what our future is imagined to be. Similar is the case of the *Mahabharata*. The *Swargaarohan Parva* is simply beyond our imagination. Here is a glimpse: The virtuous King Yudhishthir kept moving ahead without looking back at Mother Earth. He was followed by a lone dog. (Even today, on the way to Swargarohini, dogs make a sudden appearance in these snowy regions. They accompany trekkers/pilgrims for some time and then suddenly disappear. The mention of these dogs by sage Vyas proves the historic background of the *Mahabharata*.)

Yudhishthir was confronted by Indra's chariot in the sky after crossing Satopantha Lake. Indra asked Yudhishthir to be seated in his chariot but the depressed Yudhishthir said, 'I will get on the chariot only if my brothers and Draupadi, lying dead over here, accompany me. I do not wish to go to Heaven without them.' Indra smiled and said, 'O Yudhishthir, your brothers have already reached heaven. Draupadi is safe there as well.'

Here, a question arises as to how the Pandava brothers could gone to heaven when their dead bodies were lying on Earth? How was it that their human identities were intact even after death? (An effort has been made to throw more light on this topic in the chapter: Death Ceremony.) Which body did they retain? Exactly where did they go? Such questions obviously pop up in our minds.

The dog became the topic of discussion between King Yudhishthir and God Indra. Yudhishthir was reluctant to go to heaven leaving the dog on Earth. Indra then put Yudhishthir to test by asking him several questions. Indra felt gratified by the devout nature and grandeur of the King. Yama, the God of Death, appeared before Yudhishthir, abandoning his form of the dog. Thus, Yudhishthir set off for heaven in Indra's chariot.

Here, some doubts arise yet again. Yudhishthir's mortal body had still to be abandoned. Then which was the body (*kosh*), that Indra took with him? Because the Kauravas and others who had already reached heaven had acquired divine bodies, Indra, who resided there, must have also had a similarly divine body. If so, then why did he need chariots, airplanes or materialistic tools, as humans did? Yudhishthir, having reached Heaven, glimpsed Duryodhana in his divine form, but sadly, he became furious and condemned Duryodhana. At this point, the God-sage, Naarad, took the initiative and consoled Yudhishthir saying, 'Don't do that, Yudhishthir. All your previous rivalry ends once you come to heaven. You are now the beloved of the Gods, there is no place for rivalry here.'

But Yudhishthir did not wish to remain there, but to be with his brothers. Instantly, Yudhishthir witnessed heaven transformed into hell. The path to hell was crammed with algae, grass, filth, darkness and rotting flesh. Corpses, bones, insects and hair lay scattered while mosquitoes and flies buzzed everywhere. He viewed the dreadful scene in a flash of fire. He saw sinful creatures writhing in pain and from this frightful scene he could hear the moaning of Karna, Arjuna, Bhima and the other Pandavas.

The virtuous king was distressed by the terrible sight. His heart filled with wrath towards the Gods. He criticized them and told the angel with him, 'I will stay here with my brethren'. As soon as the angel returned with the King's message, God Indra arrived and the dreadful scene was completely transformed. The darkness faded away; a cool, pure and fragrant breeze began to blow. Other deities like Rudra and Aditya, gathered well. Indra, in the presence of all, said to King Yudhishthir, 'Each one has to pass through this ordeal of Hell. Good and bad deeds both bear their own fruit. He who prefers to perform good deeds first, has to suffer for the bad deeds later. You witnessed hell first as there are no sinful deeds in you. There is just one sin you committed – you lied to Drona. You had thus to suffer for that deed; now you will enjoy the eternal pleasures of heaven.' Further, Indra says to Yudhishthir, 'The rank and title you are about to gain is of excellence, like that of King Harishchandra.'

The fruits of virtue, good conduct and purity are the best. A human being may realise this only after death (this has been elaborated upon in the chapter, 'The Death Ceremony'). Though the exact whereabouts of King Yudhishthir were unknown, according to the principles laid down in the Bhagavad-Gita, he seems to have risen after death. Having gone through such a dreadful experience, Indra finally says to Yudhishthir, 'O King, this Aakaash-Ganga is the Godly River of the three worlds – Heaven, Earth and Hell. Take a dip in it first. This will end your human form (Chapter Swargarohini: 3/26). You will become free from grief and enmity.' Yudhishthir takes a dip in the divine river and abandons his body.

The connection between heaven and the galaxy is thus clear from this description. But which is that divine world? Is it attainable without renouncing the body? Is the state of bliss and divinity attainable after discarding the body? Is the divine world a well-organised community? Do they have direct control over the humans on Earth and their deeds? What is the reason behind it? Do they have a direct relation to humans – their own creations?

Achieving the divine world or heaven does not mean attaining salvation, which is considered to be a state of ultimate bliss, beyond the achievement of heaven. In salvation there is the revelation Aham Brahmasmi (I Am Brahman). The ego dies. Could the advanced Gods have programmed humans to automatically go to heaven within ten days of death?

4. HEAVEN ON EARTH

Thousands of years ago, the Gods landed on Earth from some celestial planet. Regardless of the purpose of their arrival, information about their dwelling place can be obtained from studying the ancient scriptures. Researchers are of the opinion that the Gods inhabited the remote mountains of the North Pole.

Let us take a look at some references in the *Mahabharata*. Pandu, a Kuru King, dwelled on Saptashrung mountain, with Kunti and Madri. He had lost interest in his household owing to the curse of sage Kindam. Thus he spent most of his time as a *saadhak* (follower) of the sages. One day, he got to know that a group of sages would be going to heaven and expressed his wish to go too. One of the sages discouraged King Pandu saying, 'O King, there are several obscure regions far beyond these high mountains. There are Gods' chariots buzzing all around. There is a constant hum of melodious notes. The neighbouring mountain peaks are always snow-laden, with neither trees, nor deer, nor birds. Some of the areas have incessant rain, making the ground slippery. Gods, choristers and *apsaras* dwell there, wherein they are involved in recreational activities. Pleasant parks of Kuber are situated on the banks of holy rivers. The valleys on the path are too deep to cross. It is tough not only for animals but also for birds to travel there. Only the great sages and the wind can pass through such a region. Hence it would be better for you to give up the thought of going there.' (*Mahabharata: Adi-parva A.III*)

Although this description does not indicate any specific region, it gives a clear idea of snow-laden mountain peaks, obscure mountain ranges, slippery areas and incessant rain. Also, it tells us that the region lies beyond the northern Himalayas. Which could be the region thus described?

There are similar references in the *Ramayana* as well. In the 42nd *Sarga* of *Kishkindha Kaand*, Sugreeva, while searching for Sita, says to the Vanar Sena: '...the sun sets here after having illuminated the entire region of this mortal world. O Vanaras, it is only till here that all the Vanaras can go. We are unaware of the region further, which is boundless and devoid of the sun.' Sugreeva, while describing this region also makes a mention of Gods, choristers, Meru Parvat etc. Lokmanya Tilak, in his book, *Arctic Home in the Vedas*, has set down several theories with proofs, relating to the existence of Vedic Aryans in the polar regions. Tilak started his research by considering one of the principles in the book, *Paradise Found*, by Dr. Warren as a base.

In ancient times, the North Pole was well suited to human habitatation and civilisation did exist there. Later, based on the statement of Dr. Warren that this civilisation was destroyed by the arrival of the Ice Age, Tilak concludes that ancient Indians and Europeans resided close to the North Pole in 8000 B.C. While proposing this theory, Tilak referred to various books on geology, relative archaeology, astrology, science, the *Vedas*, the *Avesta*, *Vendidad* etc., and stated there was two Ice Ages in the North Pole. Between these two Ice Ages, the polar region was suited to human habitation. The polar habitation of the sages ended in the second Ice Age. Those who survived settled in newer regions. The group that came to India settled on the banks of the river Saraswati. Once again, the Aryan civilization flourished. What was observed and remembered by the sages can be found in the *Vedas* and the *Avesta*.

Tilak's theory faced mixed reactions from Indian and foreign scholars. Recently, the German inventor, Dr. David Frauli, argued against this in his book, *The Myth of Aryan Invasion*. He opined that Aryan culture was never invasive by nature, hence establishing their own realm through invasion, was not in accordance with their principles. Dr. David concludes that it was out of the question to say the 'Aryans were the outsiders'. On due consideration, Dr. Frauli's and Tilak's observations seem apt. Why would a group of Vedic Aryans who arrived in India's north-west, from the polar regions, have waged war? Rather, the non-Aryans, impressed by the civilised Vedic lifestyle may have welcomed them. The Vedic Aryans may have narrated to the non-Aryans different stories about the Gods, divine beliefs, and thrilling memories of the polar regions. The non-Aryans on the banks of the Saraswati, impressed by the personality of the Vedic Aryans, their thinking and conduct, may have gradually adopted the Vedic culture. Later, with the drying up of the Saraswati, that group of Vedic Aryans may have advanced to the East and South. The two battles described in the *Rig-Veda* may have unfolded later.

In conclusion, Tilak's perspective that 'the Vedic Aryans had their roots in the polar regions', is quite convincing. He mentions in his Preface: 'All those inexplicable maxims from the *Vedas*, if considered from the perspective of the modern science principles, indicate about the Vedic Gods being polar-specific, or one can get clues about a polar-specific almanac; also Aryan Viejo, or the Paradise of Aryans, was here in such a region where the sun rises only once a year. The temperature of this place became adverse due to heavy snowfall, because of which the region got destroyed, and that made relocation to the South inevitable. All this has been clearly mentioned in the *Avesta*. These simple propositions, if compared to the modern-day findings from the science of stratum related to the Ice Age, the Hima-yug, and the period post the Ice Age, the Himottar-yug, then it becomes obligatory to put forth this proposition that the primitive Aryans had the polar regions of the Ice Age as their native place.'

A concept commonly found in Indian literature about the Gods who have been worshipped by Vedic sages in the *Rig-Veda* is that the days and nights of the Gods lasts six months each. Tilak states that Indian astronomers have named the North Polar Point on Earth as Meru Parvat. Further, he describes the Gods from this Meru Parvat view, with the sun beginning its journey from the sign Aries, just once in its half-revolution.

There is also mention in mythology that all Gods had Meru Parvat as their abode. Thus, the mention of day and night comprising six months each, is quite evident. Tilak cites the reference: 'There is a dictum in *Vendidad, Fargard.* 2, Paragraph 40 (paragraph 133 as per Spiegul) – *taech ayar mainyaente yat yare.* Its literal translation goes like this: 'That which is a year, is known as one day'. This dictum is similar to the one in *Taittiriya Brahmin*, an ancient Indian script. The polar peculiarity thus referenced leaves no place for doubt. There is a dialogue between Ahura Mazda and Yim, the first ever King of humans, in the latter half of the second *Fargard.* Ahura Mazda makes Yim realise that soon there would be a chilling winter and the land would be covered by snow. This would lead to the destruction of all nature. He advises to Yim to build a ship in order to preserve the seeds of all the species of plants and animals. Ahura Mazda and Yim first met in Aryan Viejo (heaven of the Iranians), in the land of Gods – the polar region. Their conversation also gives us a clearer idea about airplanes and the Gods' advanced knowledge of physics. It helps to throw light on the Gods' habitat. Yim questions Ahura Mazda, 'O virtuous Creator of Nature, how can we arrange for light in the ship to be built?' Ahura Mazda answers, 'There are artificial lamps there already; the stars, moon and sun rise and set only once a year'.

There is an explanation about *Shukla-gati* (the movement from new moon to full moon phase) and *Krishna-gati* (movement from full moon to new moon phase), in *shlokas* 24, 25 and 26 of the 8th chapter of the *Bhagavad-Gita*. The connection to divine and demonic powers is shown. However, considering the literal meaning of the *shlokas*, we can obtain proof of the Gods' inhabitance of the polar region. *Shukla-gati* means 'illuminated period'. Krishna says: 'If a soul is liberated in this period of time, then it reaches up to me'. It is to be noted that in the modern world, all the rockets sent into space by NASA during this phase were successful, whereas those launched in the *Krishna-gati* phase, were unsuccessful. Does this mean the gates of heaven open in the *Shukla-paksha* period only, between the new moon and full moon?

With respect to the soul's liberation, the sun's journey north and south, has been mentioned in the *Bhagavad-Gita*. There is night for a period of six months, when there is absolute darkness for two and a half months during the sun's journey north. If death occurred during this time, it was not possible to perform the last rites because of the Aryan belief that a dead body could not be purified without the sun's rays. Because of the lack of sunlight, the rivers stopped flowing and the plants had stunted growth. It was difficult to dispose of the dead body. It thus became customary to keep the dead body in a casket till the end of winter. Later, the corpse was treated properly when the sun began its journey north. The rivers started flowing again, birds chirped and plants grew. It was easy to perform the last rites during the sun's journey north as the sun kept moving along, and did not sink below the horizon in the polar regions during this period. Thus, this period was considered auspicious for the dead. Such souls were considered virtuous. With this in mind, Bhishma in the *Mahabharata*, while dying, held his breath till the sun began its journey north. The relation between human custom and geographical conditions is thus established.

The Gods' existence in the polar regions has been established in several books and that it was they who created the seeds for various plants and animals is evident from the conversation between Ahura Mazda and Yim. The extraterrestrial superhuman Gods inhabited the remote areas of the polar regions for a long period and their exit from these areas witnessed the beginning of heavy snowfall and freezing cold there, making it no longer suitable for human habitation. We can thus place history and civilisation in the perspective of this movement.

Lokmanya Tilak said that the scriptures of the Hindus and the Parsis are in harmony with respect to the Gods' location in the polar regions, and the exact duration of days and nights. Plutarch says that the deities of the Frisians (similar to Vishnu in Hindu mythology), slept in winter and carried out their daily chores in spring. The people of Packla Goniya were of the opinion that the Gods are imprisoned in winter and released in the spring. Irish mythology too, mention the Gods becoming ill for a period of time. The Hindus believe that there are Gods who sleep, on the day called *devashayani*, and wake after four months. Can this be a reference to the Gods' behavior in the polar regions? While there is night for six months in the region, there is absolute darkness for 100 days of those six months. Prior to this, the total period of dusk and dawn works out to four months – perhaps assumed to be the Gods' sleeping period, the time when the Sun starts its journey south.

Such examples not only reveal that the Vedic Aryans lived in the polar regions at the time of the Ice Age, around 8000 years B.C., but their direct relation to the Gods. There are many references in in the *Rig-Veda* to *Pancha Janaha*, which may have been 'five generations of humans' (perhaps the creation of the Gods), who lived in the polar regions. There is also mention in the *Mahabharata* of the creation of the Pandavas, apart from Arjuna, being the Gods' blessings. Now, how can we interpret the 'blessing' of God? Had the Gods conferred the seeds of their own creation or the formulae, upon Kunti?

It is interesting to study the detailed description of Arjuna's visit to Meru Parvat (heaven) in chapters 163 and 164 of the *Vana Parva*. Arjuna says, 'The Sun and the moon revolve around Meru Parvat every day and so do the stars'. He further explains, 'Meru Parvat wipes out the darkness with its own radiance, due to which the difference between night and day cannot be felt. A year there is formed by the amalgamation of one day and one night...' This description precisely points to the polar regions.

Tilak says in his book: 'It seems that the mention of Meru Parvat's radiance is probably the huge panorama of Aurora Borealis found over the North Pole'. Even so, it is quite possible that the Gods created artificial lighting in and around Meru Parvat. Does this seem impractical and amusing, even sensational? Then read the following description in the *Mahabharata* describing Arjuna's journey to heaven in chapter 43 of the *Vana Parva*: 'Arjuna witnessed thousands of airplanes in places that could hardly be seen by humans here on Earth. It was a place where there was no sun, moon or fire. The people there were self-illuminated. The big or small stars that could be seen over there, though large, appeared to be like tiny lamps when viewed from far. Arjuna viewed the stars which had brightness restricted to their own circumference. The thousands of choristers, spies, sages and *apsaras* present there, had a radiance about them, resembling the sun.'

In the *Mahabharata*, chapter 164, it says: 'In Heaven, there is no sunlight, heat or cold. There is no fatigue there. There is neither dust nor darkness, just a cool scented breeze that blows. There are deer and many chirping birds. Several Gods travel through the space in chariots.'

Thus, we can assume with some veracity that the Gods lived in the polar regions in the period between the two Ice Ages. These Gods may have arrived from other planets. They deliberately inhabited the remote areas of the Andes, the underground regions of cental Asia and the remote polar regions. They established their own kingdoms on Earth.

And one day, they just disappeared, leaving behind ample proof of their existence and inhabitance of Earth.

5. THE GODS' EMPIRE ON EARTH

There is a detailed description of a war between Arjuna and the Nivaatkavach demons in chapter 165 of the *Mahabharata*: 'The Nivaatkavach demons live in a *durg* (fort) in the middle of the ocean and number about 30 million. They resemble Gods in their looks, might and radiance'. Arjuna further explains to Yudhishthir, 'Indra himself placed a divine crown on my head. When I reached that place (from the skies), I saw an ocean from which gigantic waves were surging high. In that frothy ocean, there were thousands of canoes full of jewels. The ocean had large turtles, crocodiles and huge fishes.' A description follows of Arjuna's chariot descending to Earth. It is thus clear that the war was fought not in the sky but on Earth. Which then is the location on Earth – where there are (or were), large turtles in the ocean? Where could such a race of demons, who resembled the Gods in looks, might and radiance, have lived? These demons had defeated the Gods and conquered their towns and dwellings. Where were the places where the Gods lived on Earth?

It took Arjuna a few hours to reach those places so where could he have landed? In which direction could the Gods' aircrfat have taken Arjuna from the polar region? The description points to South America. Even today, there are extremely large turtles in the ocean surrounding the Galapagos Islands. The islands have remained unchanged to this day. Further north is Mexico. Handsome, robust and strong people still live there. In Mexico, there are some pyramids and an ancient observatory as well. An astronaut seated in a rocket, carved into a stone pillar, can be seen in the Mayan pyramid at

Palenque, Mexico. The Mayans were very intelligent and their civilisation advanced. It was they who passed on the astonishing legacy of calendars and mathematics to the world. Their calendar has calculations for 40 million years. That a year on Venus lasts 584 days and 365.2420 days on Earth, was known to the Mayans thousands of years ago. Today's most accurate estimatation of the Earth year is 365.2422 days. It is amazing to find that today's Venusian theory, discovered with the help of computers, was put forth by the Mayans thousands of years ago. According to them, the wheels of time reunite every 37,960 days. These ancient people were quite certain that the Gods who came to Earth had come from the cluster of stars of the sun sign Taurus. Today, when we point to the sky to indicate God, is it an extension of the belief of the ancients?

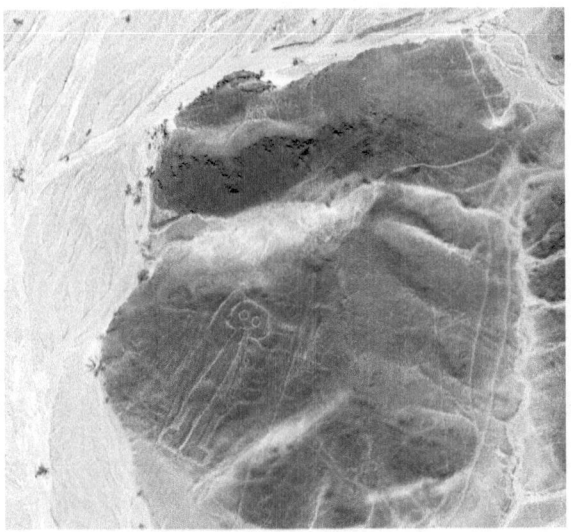

An astronaut carved into the Nazca Plateau in South America.

The evolution of the Mayan civilisation is mystifying to us. There is proof that it was an advanced civilization 10,000 years ago. The Mayans have chronicled developments in physics through symbols and diagrams in several manuscripts. This rare treasure would have proved to be a guide to the Gods' advent, their place of dwelling, as also development in physics at the time, but unfortunately Bishop Diego de Landa destroyed the Mayan manuscripts. Such fanatics, with the intention of safeguarding their hold over the community, closed the doors to ancient knowledge. The truth was suppressed. Nonetheless, truth has a way of emerging. Of the Mayan manuscripts, three were spared. The *Madrid Codex* and *Dresden Codex* explain astrnomical calculations and the orbits of Venus and the Moon. But the script uses occult signs and diagrams and hence the meaning has yet to be decoded. The meaning changes with the slightest alteration in the signs or diagrams.

However, places built by the Mayans can be seen even today. It has been proven now that the monuments in Palenque city, the pyramid in Mexico, the Chichen Itza, the Copán in Honduras and the Tickle in Guatemala, were constructed as per the Mayan calendar, meaning that a specific number of stairs in a building were completed in a specific number of days, as mentioned in the calendar. Subsequently, the plinth of the stairs was laid in the latter half of the month and then the entire temple completed within the year. Thus, not only was the whole structure built in this way but, every step was built to exact specifications in the calendar.

The Mayans suddenly disappeared, leaving behind huge structures, temples, cities and pyramids. The reason for this is not known. Western archaeologists have put forth several opinions. It has been said that atmospheric changes or a disease such as the plague might have been the reason for their disappearance. But there is no proof to substantiate this. What then could have happened all of a sudden? Was it the advent of an enemy? The

Mayan civilisation was at its peak of advancement in physics. Who then could have been a threat to them?

Had it been Arjuna who had dared to do this? This seem highly probable in the light of the description of robust people, prolonged aviation over the oceans, gigantic turtles, etc. – all of which corresponds with South America. Arjuna's and Matali's victory over the Nivaatkavach demons has been explained in detail in the *Vanaparva* of the *Mahabharata*. Were the Mayans and the Nivaatkavach the same? It is quite possible. Did they own the huge pyramid-like constructions or were those the property of the Gods? Were the enormous observatories, temples and pyramids, built according to the Mayan calendar, built by them or the Gods? Matali's reply answers these questions.

The Chichen pyramid in Itza, South America.

Arjuna fought a mystical battle with the Nivaatkavach demons. He overpowered them and entered their deserted town. Where had all the people gone? Had they settled 225 miles away – the distance between the deserted town and the new one today? The demons deserting the old town and settling some distance away is quite possible. Arjuna saw that the deserted town was vast. He was startled by the gigantic constructions, temples and tall structures studded with precious stones. He said to Matali, 'What a magnificent town these demons had developed, grander than that of the Gods!' Matali replied, 'O Paarth, it was a town of the Gods. All the huge and lavish structures were the creations of the Gods. These were taken over by the demons, who proved to be invincible to the Gods. You overpowered them all alone.'

An astronaut sculted on a 12ᵗʰ century church in Salamanc, Spain.

Does this prove the 'demons' were the Mayans? Had the demons gained know-how about civil engineering from the Gods themselves? Did Mayasur have his origin in the Mayan civilisation? He built Maya-*sabha*, mentioned in the *Mahabharata*, in a shape similar to that of the Gods' chariots. Where did he find the references and design of the Gods' chariots? Assuming the Nivaatkavach demons were the 'people' amongst the Gods in the Mayan civilisation, we can find answers to several doubts.

Suppose the US were to support a developing nation and later, that nation attacked the US, having gained the technical know-how about arms and finance. Did something similar take place 5000 years ago? During the period of the Gods' inhabitance of Earth, they fought several wars and at times even spread terror among the underdeveloped humans, of which there remains ample proof. There are references revealing that several atrocities were carried out by Gods on women on Earth. Did the Nivaatkavach and Mayans use the know-how obtained from the Gods, aginst the Gods themselves? The description of the scene between the Nivaatkavach and Arjuna makes it clear that the Gods often lost battles. How could the Gods, the Supreme Power, lose to humans? What intrigue and guile did the demons use?

The Gods had established their empire far and wide. Consider the *shloka* from *Mantrapushpanjali*: *Aum yadne na yadnamayajanta devaastaani*...then, *Aum swasti, saamraajyam, bhojjyam, swaaraajyam, vairaajyam, paarameshtyam raajyam maahaarajyamaadhipatyamayam samantaparyayi syaat... pruthivyai samudraparyantaayaa ekaraaliti*... meaning, 'Let there be the Gods' empire all over the entire Earth, over the seven oceans'. There are references to the Gods and their inhabitance on Earth in every scripture in the world and in several mythologies. Evidence of the Gods or the extraterrestrial superhumans' inhabitance of Earth, is found in every corner of the world, from Peru in South America, the plateau of Nazca, Bolivia, Mexico, America, Chile, Mid-Asia, Europe, Russia, China, Australia, to India and Africa.

Statues on Easter Island.

Thus, after a thorough study of the available evidence, we can conclude that the Gods appeared on Earth thousands of years ago and stayed for hundreds or thousands of years. Their advent left the underdeveloped humans dumbstruck. Earthly humans began assuming these extra-terrestrial astronauts to be Gods, as they rode on fire and aviated through space, causing destruction with their arms. They owned all kinds of specialized equipment; their chariots were made of transparent rock and emitted cold fire. They were the ones who established religion among humans and preached good conduct. They displayed affection towards humans and took their King into space. Human life was meaningless without them.

Is it then our destiny to await the Gods' return – generation after generation?

6. EVIDENCE OF THE GODS' INHABITANCE

It would not be wrong to state that all over the world, ancient scriptures have evidence of the Gods' inhabitance of Earth. In fact, the Gods left behind much material evidence in the form of structures, constructions, hieroglyphics, sculptures, etc. The Inca civilisation has many such evidences of the Gods' arrival; these are available even today. The Incas settled in Peru, a strip of land between the Andes mountain range and the Pacific Ocean. Lima is the capital. On a high mountain stands a trident measuring 820 feet high, carved into the rock. Because of its great height, it can easily be spotted from an airplane, even at a distance of 12 miles. The trident was a major sign for ancient astronauts. Even today, such signs or lights help in landing aircraft. Who could have formed these signs on the Nazca plateau thousands of years ago?

The Nazca plateau, 37 miles long and a mile wide, surrounded by the Andes, comes to sight after heading towards the trident, through space. It must be one of the wonders of the world. On the plateau, straight lines have been carved, running for miles. Some of the lines intersect each other while others run parallel. Strange geometric figures have been carved alongside. The lines follow a path over and down mountains. But then the lines suddenly end.

According to archaeologists, these were Inca roads. What was the purpose of having roads here? If they were for traffic going from one place to another, why do these roads reach nowhere? Not a single structure or the remains of a structure have been found. An aerial view clearly shows that the lines and figures display a code. We can assume that when the lines were carved into the rock, there were no structures or constructions there of any kind. Then why are the lines called roads? Who would build roads a mile wide but go nowhere? Why? The 820 feet-high trident can be seen when moving towards the Andes through space. A track measuring 37×1 miles can be seen going towards the trident. Who could have made such a perfect arrangement for landing spacecraft?

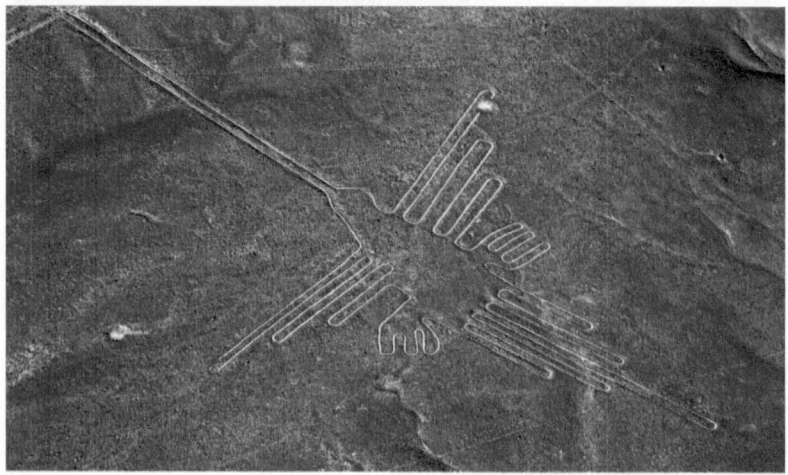

The Hummingbird made on Nazca plateau, is clearly visible from above.

There is a Mayan pyramid in Palenque, Mexico where a stairway six feet underground was found in 1935. The room below was found blocked by a shaft measuring 14×7 feet. A superb carving appears on the shaft. The Mayans carved hieroglyphics on all four surfaces of the shaft, the significance of which is still unknown to us. Nevertheless, the drawing carved on the shaft has a lot of meaning. It depicts an astronaut seated in a spaceship, seen from any side, any angle. He is seated like a driver, in a slightly bent and alert position while driving. He is seen wearing a helmet from which two pipes seem to go back. His fingers rest on some unusual buttons. His attire appears similar to 20th century astronauts. Who was this astronaut seen by the Mayans, thousands of years ago?

In Chichen, there is a huge, circular, three-storied, ancient observatory of the Mayan *lokas*. On its walls are carved pictures of flying humans. A severe earthquake occurred in Hunan province, China, after which an ancient pyramid appeared out of Kunming lake. Pictures of rockets flying into space are carved on it.

There are several caves in the world where we find pictures of Gods in costumes similar to those of modern astronauts. The Sumerian civilisation had reached great heights of technological advancement in ancient times. However, this civilisation was wiped out suddenly. These people have carved a code language and messages on bricks, with the help of arrows; but it has yet to be decoded. These Sumerians, in their calculations, noted fifteen digit number as answers. Our calculators and computers cannot display fifteen digit numbers. Similarly, electric dry cells, as old as a thousand years, have been found in the pyramids and it is still possible to generate electric current from them.

An ancient etching in Fergana, Uzbekistan, has two people – one looking straight ahead, wearing a helmet and unusual attire, and the other wearing the costume of an astronaut. The two antennae on his helmet can be clearly seen and also an oval-shaped flying saucer in space.

Similar statues with helmets can be seen in the Anthropological Museum in Mexico. A sculpture of astronauts wearing helmets has been found among Mayans ruins as well. Also found are the remains of a city called Death Valley, in America. Melted rock and gravel can be seen there even today. An erupting volcano does not possess enough heat to melt rocks, then how did these rocks melt? Can we assume primitive humans possessed advanced technology?

It is now becoming evident that thousands of years ago, humans on Earth did indeed have association with the Gods. Ravana, with their support, had progressed greatly in the field of physics. He had several chariots, of which, Pushpak is the most famous. Wariyapola in Sri Lanka is situated close to Kandy. Wariyapola in Sinhalese means 'place for plane landing'. Dr. Madhusudan Chansarkar, in his Marathi book, *Saptasagaratil Sri Lankecha Shodh* (Search for Sri Lanka in the Seven Seas), has thrown light on the battle between Rama and Ravana, the advancement made by Ravana in physics, as well as the political drama at the time in Sri Lanka. There is mention of Indrajit, Ravana, and others, having fought wars from aircrafts. In those battles, they used destructive weapons which worked on electric, solar, wind and magnetic energy. More dangerous weapons than atomic ones existed. It has been mentioned in several versions of the *Ramayana* that the war involved the armies of many countries and the Gods as well. Ravana proved formidable against the Gods and therefore, Indra supported Rama in the battle, providing him with an airforce.

Figures seen on Nazca Plateau.

Dr. Chansarkar also states in his book that the weapons used in the war were so advanced that both Sri Lanka as well as the southern tip of India became submerged in the ocean. The effect of the weapons led to radiation spreading to three-fourths of Sri Lanka. Also, he states that God Hanuman carried the Dronagiri Parvat not through the air but in his spaceship. It was because he travelled in this way that he reached the Himalayas and returned in time. Even today, in Galle (Sri Lanka), Dronagiri looks as though a Himalayan mountain has been uprooted from a mountain range. A narrow, northern section lies in the ocean while a detached part stands on land. The vegetation on these mountains differ from that found in Sri Lanka.

Several such tales provide evidence of the role of the Gods and prove that, while establishing religion on Earth, they intended to safeguard their hold on the planet and maintain supremacy. Brahmadev, in the 52nd *sarga* of the *Ramayana*, after seeing Sita's abduction with divine vision, says, 'Now we have accomplished our mission'. He was pleased that Sita's abduction would distress the great sages and confirm Ravana's end at Rama's hands.

The *Mahabharata* reflects politics among the Gods as well. Non-Aryans inhabited Khandava-van with cobras, peacocks, wolves, birds, demons and evil doers. They were all blessed by Indra. Today, the US maintains amicable political relations with Pakistan since it provides them with a firm foothold on the Asian continent. Powerful countries prefer to remain oblivious to the non-aggressive and tolerant populations, concerned simply with their own supremacy. Did the Gods resort to similar politics in Khandava-van? At any hint of opposition, Lord Indra would appear in his chariot and defeat the enemy. No one dared oppose Khandava-van.

And yet, the tale of Krishna and Arjuna's victory in Khandava-van is well-known. How then were the Gods defeated? The mere idea of defeating an unconquerable Supreme Power sounds impractical. But the fact that the Nivaatkavach demons, Krishna and Arjuna, defeated the powerful forces of the Gods, means the Gods who had arrived on Earth were distinct from the Supreme Power.

Consider some examples from various mythological stories: the Madi-Moru is an African tribe; it is said in their mythology that human initially inhabited heaven and frequently commuted to Earth. But, a blue bird broke the ladder to heaven. The Zulus are another African tribe; the word *zulu* means 'heaven'. According to their Zulu tradition, their ancestors came directly from heaven, hence they refer to their country as 'a nation of heavenly humans'.

Derinkuyu is an ancient, multi-level, underground city in the Nevsehir Province of Turkey.

It is believed by the Masai that the Gods created the moon and stars; it was they who first created plant life on Earth, after which they introduced animals. Rugaba is the name of the original God of the Ziba tribe in Tanzania. According to them, Rugaba inhabits distant space, not Earth. Since there was darkness everywhere, he created the first human being on Earth. According to Bushongo (Congo) mythology, a huge, fair-skinned human, Bumba, came to Earth; he chose a human as King, and returned to space. *Bumba* is similar to *Brahma* in Indian mythology. Is it just a coincidence?

Mongulala, another South American tribe has a fascinating history, recorded from the time when the Gods left Earth. Ina, their Prince, ordered his subjects to chronicle all events henceforth. From then, i.e. since approximately 12,000 years ago, the tribe has assiduously followed the wishes of their Prince. We thus know that farming was not practiced by humans in those times, nor did they wear clothes. Any social or political system was unheard of. Suddenly, one day, flying chariots were seen in the sky; they emitted tremendous flashes of light (like Indra's chariot), and the ground shook. At first, 130 families of Gods appeared on Earth. They made arrangements to live underground as well. They ruled Earth, imparted knowledge to the people and taught them a system. In short, they were instrumental in establishing civilisation. But then, one day, they left Earth and returned to the skies in their chariots, foretelling impending disaster. However, they assured Ina that they would reappear on Earth when the human race was in trouble. Earth witnessed two major calamities twelve years later – there was a cold wave that spread over the Earth, but in some places it was searingly hot. Winds blew at enormous speeds, uprooting trees. The ecosystem of the Earth was disturbed. Most humans lay buried under piles of snow. It was thanks to the Gods that the human race was saved from extinction.

The Mongulala community has preserved this written history, which is similar to Dr. Warren's theory. In his book, based on geology and titled, *Paradise Found*, he states that in even more ancient times, the polar region in the north was suited to human existence and had settlements. Further, that human civilisation was destroyed due to the sudden advent of the Ice Age. This happened nearly 8,000 years ago.

Tatunka Nara from the Mongulala civilization, has written that the Gods did reappear on Earth as they had promised. Once again, their aircraft could be seen flying in the sky, but there were hardly any humans left on Earth to welcome them. This is reminescent of a *shloka* from the *Bhagavad-Gita*: *Paritraanaaya saadhunaam vinashaayacha dushkrutaam dharmasansthapanarthaaya sambhavami yege yuge ll* (Whenever dharma is weakened and adharma gets stronger, I take birth. I take birth in every era to protect good, eradicate evil and establish the rule of dharma).

Similar to the mythology of other nations, the *Vedas* assert much the same thing. It has been said in *19-20 Agnimarut Palupad-sukta* in the first *Mandal* of the *Rig-Veda*, that enlightened immortals dwell in paradise, in space. Rishi states in *Sutra III*, that Ashwinikumar created a chariot with three wheels that could fly in the sky. The 59th *sukta* in the 1st *Mandal* supports the proposition that the Gods' inhabited the polar region of Earth: 'O Fire Element, you are the one who rules Dyava Pruthvi, you are the one who is placed to the head of Dyu-loka and in the center of the Earth, you have been created by Gods for the Aryans in the form of fire'.

The 116th *Ashwinikumar Sukta* mentions: 'O Ashwinikumar, you, who are fully equipped with horses that fly high in the sky and run at high speed on land, defeated thousands of enemy forces in violent battle. With the help of amphibian ships (flying in air as well as on water), you saved Bhujyu who was shoved mercilessly by Tugra into the ocean, as also those dying people who sacrificed their wealth recklessly.'

The Rishis say in *Ashwinikumar Prashasti-Sukta* 118, 'O Ashwinikumar, may your chariot, which is swifter than the human mind, which has three shafts, which is equipped with Shyen birds, which is rich and valuable, and which has a speed greater than wind come to us' and 'O Ashwinikumar, please come to us in your triangular three shafted, three wheeler, smooth chariot' (1.118.2). Agastya Maitrawaruni addressing Ashwinikumar, once again states in the *183rd Sukta*: 'O valorous Ashwinikumar, please come to our abode in such a chariot equipped with three wheels and three wings, resembling the bird Supaksha'. In the previous *Sukta*, it says: 'O Ashwinikumar, you created a self-operated ship equipped with wings that could propel itself in an ocean, in which you set off to Dev-loka (territory of Gods)'.

In the 34th *shloka* of first *Mandal*, there is more evidence of the flying chariots of the Gods: 'O Ashwinikumar, arriving in a three-wheeled triangular chariot, what are these wheels and seats made up of...? O Ashwinikumar, consume Somaras, seated in the delightful, sunlit, well-fuelled *ghrutayukta* chariot appearing before dawn.'

Does *ghrutayukta* in the above *shloka* mean oil or fuel? This question, posed by the sages, clearly show they were unacquainted with the technology used by the Gods. On the one hand, they mention fuel, yet on the other hand, they mention a 'sunlit' chariot. Does the *Sukta* indicate that the 'sunlit chariot' operated on solar energy?

In the *Suktas* about Ashwinikumar, there is repeated mention of a triangular, three-wheeled chariot. It must be pointed out here that the vehicle which landed on the moon had three wheels and was quite similar to this description. There are also several references in the *Rig-Veda* about the Gods' chariots and their frequent contacts, as well as the exceptional capability of those chariots and their advanced technology. *Sukta 119* says: 'O valiant Ashwinikumar, like a mechanic repairs an old chariot, you have conferred new life upon the frail Vandan. Pleased by the *mantras* of poet Ushanus, you pulled him out of the mother's womb.'

Now, how was he removed from the womb? By performing a caesarian section? Does that seem impossible? An overall review of ancient literature makes one thing clear, irrespective of whether they were advanced or primitive, ancient humans were definitely aware of advanced physics. How were they acquainted with these concepts when they were otherwise underdeveloped? Was it the doing of the Gods?

How did Gandhari deliver 100 sons and a daughter? Consider this scene from the *Mahabharata*: when the pregnant Gandhari pounded her stomach, a mass of flesh emerged. Hearing Gaandhari's wails, Maharshi Vyas arrived on the spot. He, with the help of a few experts, cut the mass of expelled flesh into 101 pieces and placed them in different containers, adding some specific chemicals. The containers were opened after a certain period of time. Thus were born all the Kauravas, all of whom were of the same age. Duryodhana was considered to be the eldest simply because his container was opened first.

Which process could have been adopted at that time? Could it have been cloning? Human evolution according to Darwin's theory is well known, implying that primitive humans were not as advanced as modern man. If this is assumed to be true, how did modern theories exist in those ancient times? Who introduced them and how were they available in written form? Does it mean humans wrote them down without having any experience of them?

The similarity between the Sumerian Goodess Inanna and the Indian Goddess Durga is striking and clear.

In the *Old Testament*, there is a description of the Gods, or their messengers, arriving with loud sounds and clouds of smoke. Ezekiel describes the Gods' luminous chariot gliding through the sky, creating a sandstorm in the desert. He also mentions several other vehicles emerging from the Gods' gigantic sky-chariot. Ezekiel had contact with God, with whom he had a dialogue. His descriptions are amazing. Once Moses asked God, 'Why don't you make an appearance?' To which God replied, 'You will not be able to bear it. If a human sees my face, he would cease to exist.'

The legend of Tiahuanaco states that a woman named Ariana arrived in a gleaming spaceship to become Mother of the Earth. In the epic *Gilgamesh*, in the Sumerian civilisation, there is a comprehensive narration about the Gods' advent and inhabitance of Earth. Surprisingly, there is great similarity between the story of the origin of the world as mentioned in this epic and in Genesis.

The *Padma Purana*, an ancient Indian scripture, contains information about the origin of the world. Is it just coincidence that what is in the *Padma Purana*, written thousands of years ago, resembles today's Big Bang theory? There is a whole chapter on the subject, which mentions that prior to the creation of nature, there was a giant golden egg that broke. One part of it went shooting upwards and the other fell down and shattered. From this were formed the stars, planets and water. Thus, ancient mythology and scriptures have attempted to chronicle the Gods' advent on Earth and the world's genesis. These facts have been recorded for posterity as well as expressed through the construction of commemorative structures. If we observe with an open mind, without prejudice, much can be gained from the available data which can only enrich our lives. When humans give up a one-sided and dogmatic approach to viewing things, harmony can prevail.

To summarise, in ancient times, the Gods or superhumans came to Earth and inhabited it with some specific purpose. Perhaps it was they who created modern man. They established religion. They also paid periodic visits to Earth and built huge dwellings in several places. They exhibited a certain level of intolerance while promoting their social system among undeveloped humans. At times, they performed atrocities too. Tales of Indra and Ahilya are well-known. There is also mention of how the Gods debased women. The book of Enoch contains a small description of a space journey undertaken by him. When Enoch asked God about his fate, God replied, 'I cannot tell you since I do not know the future'.

This seems to denote that the Gods were not omniscient; they erred. It is obvious that the humans, astonished by the alien astronauts' or the Gods' knowledge of physics, began believing them to be the Supreme Power. They sought their assistance and became devotional towards them. One day, after reassuring them they would return, the Gods bid farewell to Earth, never to return.

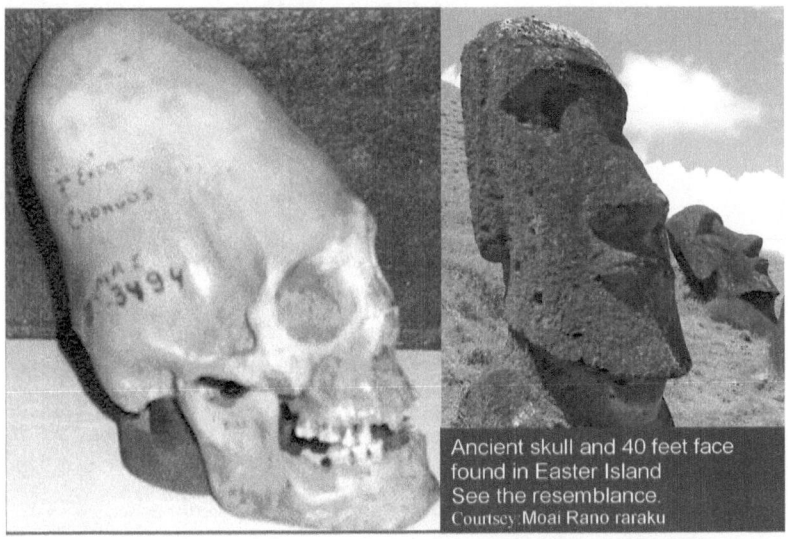

Ancient skull and 40 feet face found in Easter Island See the resemblance. Courtsey Moai Rano raraku

An ancient human skull and 40-foot carved face found on Easter Island. The resemblance between the two is unmistakable.

While human beings flourished materially, their desire for the Gods' return never diminished. Even in today's sinful and corrupt times, the virtuous and devout yearn for their reappearance. However, given the current situation, perhaps even the Gods from heaven will not be able to uplift decadent humanity. Who can do that? Who can establish morality on Earth?

We need not despair; the all-pervasive God, the Supreme Spirit, the Almighty, undoubtedly still exists. The theory that the Gods were extraterrestrials has been proved, with evidence. But these extraterrestrials from boundless space cannot be called Gods or the Almighty referred to by the sages and saints. The Gods refered to in the early chapters refers to those astronauts who arrived from space as adominant race. We can co-relate the existence of such Gods from the ancient scriptures from all over the world. With its population of 33 crore Gods, their chariots, and the *Rig-Veda* etc., India has a fascinating and awe-inspiring history of Gods.

7. THE DISPUTATION

There are diverse opinions on whether the Gods were extraterrestrial superhumans or not. That such Gods lived on Earth some thousands of years ago, was the theory put forth by archaeologist, Erich von Däniken, along with ample evidence. He also asserted that the roads of the Incas, the pyramids of the Mayans and Egyptians, were the creations of these Gods. He gives a detailed explanation for his contention. However, there are many critics of this theory. Däniken had been accused of presenting false evidence. His mendacity had come to light several times before.

Archaeologists and scientists credit the building of the pyramids to humans. They claim the pyramids were built in three ways. In the first method, ramps of huge logs were built and greased with oil and water. Causeways may also have been built around this. Then huge stone blocks were pulled over the ramp. Ten workers would have sufficed for this mammoth task. In the second method, huge wooden cranes were used to lift 2.5 tonne stone blocks. To balance the crane, they placed even heavier weights. This made it easy to lift 2.5 tonnes. However, this method was disproved since there were no trees in Egypt suited to making such huge wooden cranes. The third method used pulleys to lift the blocks. Pulleys were widely used in ships in those times. Today, scientists are still studying these possibilities. Though we cannot be sure of the method of construction, we can assume they were the work of humans and not the Gods.

Tiahuanaco is one of the deserted towns left by the Inca. It stands in a dilapidated condition. In the middle of the town, there is a huge idol of a deity. Coded information is carved on the idol. Dr. Hubijar theorised that about 27,000 years ago, a large satellite revolved around Earth and made 425 revolutions in 288 days. One day, it was pulled towards Earth and exploded. Its parts scattered in space, but one piece kept moving in its orbit around Earth; this is our Moon. This theory, however, was contradicted by Dr. Robert Shepherd, who said that assuming Earth orbited around the Sun in 288 days, as per Kepler's 3rd rule, it would be too close to the Sun, i.e. where Mercury is. It was the Ice Age 27,000 years ago. Could an Ice Age have occured on Earth if it was in such proximity to the Sun? Did Earth complete its revolution around the Sun much faster then than the 365 days it takes to do so today? Däniken puts forth a contrary theory: how could the satellite moving around Earth maintain a safe distance from both the Sun and Earth?

Däniken presents his theory about Venus with reference to the ancient Egyptians. He questions how the Egyptians could prepare a calendar using Venus as a reference, when Venus is seen very dimly from Egypt. Dr. Robert Shepherd answers that barring the North Pole, Venus is seen in the same luminosity all over Earth. Däniken, while mentioning the mathematical prowess of the Mayans, says that a solar year on Earth is of 365 days duration and 584 days on Venus. Dr. Shepherd objects, saying the Venus year comprises of 225 days, not 584.

In another hypothesis, Däniken cites the Nazca plateau as evidence. In South America are located the Andes mountains. The Nazca desert spreads 1,400 miles parallel to the Pacific Ocean. Above it, an area 37 miles long and 15 miles wide, has strange artistic work done by the Nazca people. This plateau is also known as Pampa Colorada and the Red Plain. The Nazca civilization flourished between 200 B.C. and 300 A.D. Recently, scientists excavated red rocks from the plateau and studied them. It was observed that instead of sand, it was a pale coloured soil.

There is another theory that the strange lines on the plateau and the carved pictures of animals, might have served as a guide for those coming from outer space. But most scholars are of the opinion that it might have been a religious place for the Incas. It must have taken them hundreds of years to build it. 'The enormity of the Nazca plateau, huge carved pictures of strange straight lines, giant lizards, spiders, monkeys, llama, dogs, and humming birds might have been made to serve as a guide for the aliens,' wrote James Mozley in *Fate* (1855). During the 1960s, Lewis Powell and Jack Brazier shared this concept with the public. While it was thrilling, there was no trace of any divine chariots or common spacecraft having landed on the Nazca plateau and damage caused by friction from such landings. There is no evidence of this.

Yet questions are still raised as to how primitive Red Indians and ancient Incas could have created such masterpieces. Some scholars opine that these masterly creations did not require high-end technology, just the expertise of the artists. A few researches feel the lines on the Nazca plateau could have been made for running races. G. Von Brenig has found footprints there. Others consider it to have been some religious place for public prayers, like Mecca.

To summarise, even though the history of the pyramids, the mathematical prowess of the Mayans, the theory of Venus, the lines at Nazca, are all astonishing, we need not relate them to extraterrestrials. On the other hand, the historical references to the Gods, as in the *Mahabharata* and other mythology, carved pictures of aliens wearing helmets, cannot be ignored either. Instead of presenting thrilling and revolutionary theories, it is necessary to research this subject further with a rational attitude.

The purpose of this book, up to this point, has revolved around the idea that the Gods may or may not have been extraterrestrials. They may or may not have created an advanced human. But one thing is certain, ancient human civilisation leaves us confounded. Civilisations flourish, peak, and then spiral into a downfall. Then all its achievements, evidence, sculptures, murals, and monuments, become precious treasures and matters of self-esteem. The truth lies hidden within them. This has happened for thousands of years, and will continue to do so. We must only continue our search.

But now we enter the realm of the Supreme Power or the Almighty, the *Para Brahma*. This realm is divine, transcendental, beautiful, blissful and full of vigour. Human language falls short in describing this kingdom. In fact, experience rather than words is of the utmost importance in this realm of Supreme Power. This minuscule effort is an attempt to study this aspect from a rational point of view so that the Almighty's kingdom, when understood by the intellect, can undeniably change our lives. This is an effort to make the intellect understand that which appeals to the soul. This book does not claim to impart any kind of knowledge about the divine dimensions of the Almighty, but only to explore it by collating several links.

Thus, without again looking back at the Gods from space, we now enter the kingdom of bliss, which can transform our lives into a beautiful and healthy existence.

PART II
EMPIRE OF THE SUPREME POWER

8. FORMATION OF THE KNOWN WORLD

It is valuable to learn about the vast world formed by Him. Astronomers have presented many theories regarding the characteristics of the universe. Considerable reserach has been done into time and space as well. The universe, composed of matter, has millions of planets – some gaseous, others of differing densities. There are hardly any planets which have an atmosphere.

With this background, there is a brief but precise indication of the formation of the world and its Creator, in ancient Indian literature. Understanding the *shlokas* as formulae is not possible through objective study. It requires a different perspective altogether. In the 7th chapter of the *Bhagavad-Gita*, the Almighty says, 'This world of mine (*trigunaatmak* or threefold), is divided based on eight aspects – earth, water, fire, air, space, mind, intellect and ego. This is my "lower nature". But, there is another different, living, exalted world of mine that has enveloped this lower nature. Since the bodily elements are formed out of these two worlds, I am the reason for its origin as well as its end. Nothing can be separated from me in principle. This whole world is interwoven within me just like pearls get strung in a necklace.' The Almighty adds, 'Attaining knowledge of my nature (form) and consequently the formation of the known as well as the unknown world, is a rare occurrence.'

There is clear mention of the formation and structure of this world in several ancient Hindu scriptures. We can consider the reference in the *Bhagavad-Gita* by Maharshi Vyas, according to which, the life of this world lasts 100 days and 100 nights. These 100 days are not earth years but refers to the days of Lord Brahma (one day equals 4,320,000,000 earth years). There is a brief mention of this formula in the 17th and 18th *shlokas* of chapter 18 of the *Bhagavad-Gita*. After one day and one night of Brahma, the entire planetary system comes to an end.

According to Vedic cosmology, there are 14 planetary levels, the descending order of which is as follows: 1. *Satyalok*, 2. *Tapolok*, 3. *Janalok*, 4. *Maharlok*, 5. *Swarlok*, 6. *Bhuvarlok*, 7. *Bhurlok*, 8. *Atal*, 9. *Vital*, 10. *Sutal*, 11. *Talaatal*, 12. *Mahatal*, 13. *Rasaatal*, and 14. *Paataal*.

Below these 14 planetary levels is *Pitrulok*, below which is *Naraklok* (Hell). This planetary system has 27 more sub-divisions, containing hundreds and thousands of planets. It is stated that the level of consciousness of souls sent to *Naraklok*, is extremely low.

Space and time have ever fascinated the hiuman mind.

As per the *Bhagavad-Gita*, our Earth exists in the planetary system of *Bhurlok/Bhumandal*. This planetary system sub-divided into seven parts – *Jambu, Plaksha, Salmali, Kusha, Krauncha, Shaka,* and *Pushkara*. It looks like a disc from a distance. Books like the *Bhagavad-Gita*, though spiritual, include several astronomical theories. A few examples are: in *shloka* 5.21.19, the Sun, in its orbit through *Bhumandal*, traverses a distance of 95,100,000 *yojanas* (ancient Indian unit of measurement), at a speed of 2,000 *yojanas* and two *kosas* (16,004 miles), in a moment. When converted, it works out to 760,800,000 miles, completiing one revolution of 16,004 miles per second, which is very close to modern scientific calculations.

While mentioning the exact age of the Sun and its lifespan, the *Bhaagwat* states that the Sun manifested 155,521,960,853,098 years ago and will degenerate 155,518,039,146,902 years from now. 'The part of the Earth facing the Sun will have day and its opposite side will have night', was mentioned in the *Bhaagwat* thousands of years ago in *shlokas* 5.21.8-9, long before Aristotle said so. Likewise, the *Bhaagwat* also points to the reference of Einstein's theory of relativity in *slokas* 9.3, 30-32, which narrates how one spaceman went to the highest planetary system and stayed there for 20 months. When he returned to Earth, 116,640,000 years had passed. We also have the story of King Kakudmi, who arrived at the highest level to find Lord Brahma engaged in listening to a musical performance by the Gandharvas and did not have a moment to speak to him. Kakudmi waited. At the end of the performance, he offered his obeisance to Lord Brahma and submitted his long-standing desire. Lord Brahma laughed loudly and said to Kakudmi: 'O King, all those whom you may have decided within the core of your heart to accept as your son-in-law, have passed away in the course of time. Twenty-seven *chatur-yugas* have already passed. Those upon whom you may have decided are now gone, and so are their sons, grandsons and other descendants. You cannot even hear about their names.'

The *Bhaagwat* also states that this universe is divided into specific *yugas* (time periods) and exists in time cycles. The four time periods during each cycle of the universe are:

1. *Satya Yuga*

2. *Treta Yuga*

3. *Dwapar Yuga*

4. *Kali Yuga*

The duration of each *yuga*, as outlined in the *Bhaagwat* (3.11.19) is:

1. *Satya Yuga* = 4800 *years* x 360 = 17,28,000 earth years

2. *Treta Yuga* = 3600 x 360 = 12,96,000 earth years

3. *Dwapar Yuga* = 2400 God years x 360 = 8,64,000 earth years

4. *Kali Yuga* = 1200 God years x 360 = 4,32,000 earth years.

We are currently living in the second half of *Kali Yuga*.

Similarly, the concept of *lokas* (i.e. planetary systems), is presented in a different way in Indian mythology. *Lokas* also mean a section or division of the universe. In this context, the universe is assumed to consist of three divisions: Heaven, Earth and the nether world. Some scholars regard Hell as one of the three *lokas*, instead of the nether world. It is said that the Sun, Lord Vishnu, and Lord Shiva, are the three deities who preside over the three *lokas*.

There are seven other *lokas*, apart from these three:

1. *Bhur-lok* denotes Earth.

2. *Bhuvar-lok* is the space between Earth and the Sun.

3. *Swar-lok* is the Heaven of Lord Indra, located between the Sun and the North Pole.

4. *Mahar-lok* is where Bhrugu Rishi and others reside.

5. *Jana-lok* is the residing place of Brahma's three sons –
Sanak, Sananda and Sanatkumar.

6. *Tapo-lok* is the residence of ascetics.

7. *Satya-lok* or *Brahma-lok* is the residence of Lord Brahma.

Vedanta believes that human beings attain salvation when
they reach *Sapta-lok.*

According to Early Indian scientists, at the end of every
era, the three *lokas* – *Bhur-lok, Bhuvar-lok* and *Swar-lok* get
destroyed. The last three *lokas* i.e. *Jana-lok, Tapo-lok* and
Satya-lok get destroyed at the end of Brahma's life. But the
Mahar-lok of the *Sapta* (seven) *rishis,* is eternal and cannot be
destroyed. However, *Mahar-lok* becomes unfit for residence
due to the heat produced during the destruction of first three
lokas.

Other names of these *lokas* are *Pruthvi* (Earth), *Antariksha*
(space), *Swarg* (Heaven), *Madhya-Vibhag, Janmasthan*
(birthplace), *Punya-praasad* and *Satyalok.* There is a mention of
eight *lokas* in the *Saankhya Darshana* and the *Vedanta Darshana.*
These *lokas* are:

1. *Brahma-lok,* the residence of Gods of high rank.

2. *Pitru-lok,* where ancestors reside.

3. *Som-lok,* consisting of the moon and planets.

4. *Indra-lok,* the residence of Lord Indra and the deities.

5. *Gandharva-lok,* where angelic beings reside.

6. *Rakshas-lok,* the home of demons.

7. *Yaksha-lok,* the residence of demigods.

8. *Pishaccha-lok,* the place of spirits.

Let us interpret these *lokas* (planetary systems), mentioned in ancient writings of India.

a. These *lokas* did not exist on Earth, but in space.

b. The exact location of some of the *lokas* has been specified. For example, *Swar-lok* (Lord Indra's residence), is situated between the Sun and the North Pole. Did Lord Indra and the deities come to Earth from there? Did the virtuous King Yudhishthir, along with Lord Indra, go to this *Swar-lok*?

c. Except for *Mahar-lok*, the others get destroyed.

d. Lord Brahma is not immortal. There is an end to his life.

To summarise: *lokas* signify divisions in space and this was known to the early *rishis*. Lord Brahma, Lord Indra and the other deities were considered mortal, too. Nevertheless, the ultimate controller of this universe, the Almighty, never dies. It is quite evident from the above, that the Gods we worship are different from the *Para Brahma* principle.

Although the Gods are mortal, their bodies were certainly different from earthly humans; they were of some superior form. They seem to have been of a different dimension altogether, noble and grand. Their inhabitance could have been on some visible or invisible planet in space, somewhere between the Sun and the North Pole. They could have visted Earth from there, thousands of years ago, riding strange aircraft. Even today, the four parallel stars moving in the belt between the Sun and the Pole Star, are known as *Swargadwar* (Door to Heaven). Is it a mere co-incidence?

There are also some assumptions we can make regarding the seven *rishis* who resided in *Mahar-lok*. There were seven different *Sapta-rishis* in each *manvantar* (reign), and 14 *manvantars* in all. This means there were 98 *rishis* in all. These *Sapta-rishis* are divided into two lists as follows:

First list: 1. Kashyap, 2. Atri, 3. Bharadwaj, 4. Vishwamitra, 5. Gautam, 6. Jamadagni and 7. Vasishtha.

Second list: 1. Marichi, 2. Atri, 3. Angiras, 4. Pulatsya, 5. Pulaha, 6. Hrutu and 7. Vasishtha.

Currently, we live in *Vaivaswat manvantar*. This reign is considered to be that of the *Sapta-rishis* Vasishtha, Kashyap, Atri, Jamadagni, Gautam, Vishwamitra and Bharadwaj, who are the prophets of the reign. Humans, Dev, the *Sapta-rishis* and Lord Indra, were considered the ultimate authorities, in ancient times. Most humans are linked to the *Sapta-rishis*. However, nearly all humans have forgotten their association with the *rishis*. But in India, even today, every family belongs to a pre-ordained clan, which is linked to a *rishi*. Indian astronomers indicate the residence of the *Sapta-rishis* in space as the seven prominent stars revolving around the North Star. Could this cluster of stars have been the residence of the *Maharshis* (sages) mentioned in *Mahar-lok*?

It is also believed that all human lives on Earth are under the control of these *rishis*. Were these learned sages then the ones who came to Earth thousands of years ago? It is believed they have an invisible presence even today. They advise devout souls and inspire those who wish to accomplish their desired goals. Each *rishi* attempts to develop purity in the families linked to his clan.

The complexity of this topic of the *Sapta-rishis* is perhaps beyond the common man. Nonetheless, it might be an undisputable truth of this world. From the knowledge given to us in ancient Indian philosophy, the enormity of the known or manifested world, can easily be judged. But we cannot travel beyond to the unmanifested worlds. It is rarely possible to realise the higher level principles that supersede the lower level. Nonetheless, there are several ways to realise the Almighty, the Supreme Power. We will discuss how.

9. THE TEN INCARNATIONS

Ten incarnations of God is an age-old notion in India. Thousands of years ago, Lord Krishna proclaimed in the *Bhagavad-Gita: Paritranaaya Sadhunam Vinaashayacha Dushkritam Dharmasanstha-panarthaya Sambhavami Yuge* Yuge (I come through the ages to eradicate evil and to meet the saints and ascetics.)

Indians firmly believe the controller of this universe can appear in any form, anywhere, without shattering his originality. This belief exists in most religions but Hinduism believes strongly in incarnations. Incarnation as a doctrine of belief has firm roots in Mahayana Buddhism as well. Kapilavastu, is the birthplace of Buddha, considered to be the incarnation of Bodhisattva, in his previous birth. The Dalai Lamas in Tibet are considered to be incarnations of God. The notion exists among the Persians as well. The Shia Muslims are firm believers in reincarnation. They allege that Ali and his two sons were Gods' elected *Imams* or saints. There is a difference of opinion over the number of Muslim *Imams* – some say seven, others twelve.

The Muslim religion believes divine power exists and comes to man's aid in difficult times. The Zoroastrians believed their King possessed divine power. The Egyptians were conviced there was a godly component in the royal dynasty. The Greeks, however, did not believe in incarnation but that the Almighty helps mankind in times of crisis by taking any form. Jesus Christ is considered a prophet, not an incarnation of the Almighty. In a nutshell, all religions and faiths across the world strongly believe that the divine power had a presence on Earth in human form, for whatever reasons.

The Saankhya system in India, and Jean Baptiste Lamark and Charles Darwin in the West, gave us the theory of evolution. Darwin stated that the world originated from water. Some scientists assume there were two eras – *Matsya-kalpa* (fish era), and *Kurma-kalpa* (tortoise era) There is believed that the Divine Power took the human form in *Matsya-kalpa* but that the human body structure at the beginning of the era, was quite different from what it is today. In short, some researchers and theologists believe that evolution was behind the ten incarnations of God concept.

Conversely, Indian mythology portrays the virtues of the divine power in embodied forms which appear rational. The Divine Spirit descends in three ways: *transmigration, possession and emanation*. In transmigration, the soul imbibes divine virtue through repeated reincarnations but there is no suggestion of divine power. During possession, the Divine Power assumes a form, but only for a particular reason and for a limited time. Such a form cannot be called an incarnation as it is temporary. During emanation, the Divine Element descends into a soul and the soul becomes divine. Divine Power originates in such a soul, which means that an evolved soul is different from the Almighty. The Almighty in human form does not occur during emanation. Nevertheless, it can be assumed it is an element of the divine form.

It is thus quite evident that the three concepts – evolution-generated reincarnation, temporary infusion of the Divine Element, and generation of the Divine Spirit in a soul, are completely different from *incarnation*. The evolving soul does not possess any divine virtues where the ten incarnations are supported by the theory of evolution. The process of evolution implies a gradual, vertical progression, whereas descent implies the Divine Element descending into a soul. The Almighty has no attributes but that He *can* descend, with attributes, forms the basis of incarnation. Incarnation implies Brahma's descent into a soul. Vedic doctrine asserts incarnation cannot happen without a reason.

Ralph Waldo Emerson, the American philosopher and essayist, said that an incarnation is like the foam on the waves of the ocean. The waves collide against each other, resulting in the formation of foamy water. Similarly, the collective effort of great souls produces incarnations. The revered Pandurang Shastri Athavle tells us: 'Incarnation is the result of consistent efforts and acts. God does not descend for holy men because 'we' consider them to be so, but because 'God' considers them to be holy souls. There is much effort on the part of these saints behind the divine element's descent. God dislikes complaining people. He supports those who endeavour for the betterment of society.'

The *Upanishads* have a highly developed and mature approach to the theory of incarnation – that collective effort is needed for life's overall progress. When it falls short, *Rajoguna* (lust) overrides other aspects and materialistic desires keep multiplying. This results in intense *Tamoguna* (hot-temper). The combination of these two qualities steadily attacks *Satvaguna* (morality, peace, contentment and equality). The weakening of *Satvaguna* leads to the Divine Power descending on Earth as the regulating authority, for collaborative effort. This empowers *Satvaguna*. The atoms of *Satvaguna* get purified, discrepancies disappear and a collaborative struggle is established.

Thus the Almighty says in the *Bhagavad-Gita: I come through ages to eradicate evil and to meet the saints and ascetics.* The rhythm of society is prone to anarchy, therefore the Divine Element or the Almighty has to appear again and again to set right the system. This is the philosophy behind the ten incarnations.

The above interpretation clearly indicates that the metaphors or symbolic representations in the form of *Matsya* (fish), *Kurma* (tortoise), and *Varaha* (swine), used in the ten incarnations, do not possess any virtues, just as transmigration, possession and emanation do not exist. This means that the early Indian philosophers did not elucidate incarnation with reference to the evolution of souls. Rather, they developed a more advanced, wider and clearer perspective. If we fail to understand this, we will keep assuming these symbolic narrations to be true stories.

10. BRAHMA: THE ONLY REALITY

Shankaracharya, born in the 7th century, experienced total bliss while in a state of meditation. The words he uttered were, *'Brahma Satya Jaganmitthyaa'* (I am Brahma. That is the only truth in this world and rest, unreal. I am that Almighty. I am the only one residing in each soul.) Similar was the experience of Raman Maharshi.

The Hebrew word *Yahweh* implies 'I am that I am'. The same has been the experience of all those souls who have attained a state of self-realisation. Sages and *yogis* seek spirituality, whereas scientists and researchers seek the reality of this world and the causes of its creation, externally. There are many limitations to this. Knowledge of astronomy is still in its infancy when compared with the vastness of the universe. It took thousands of years for scholars to understand electrons and protons in matter, and advance to nano-technology. Man sees only a tiny portion of the maze as his intellect develops. Thus, it would not be justified to assume that no divine power is responsible for creation.

Lord Krishna explicitly tells Arjuna in the *Bhagavad-Gita*: 'This entire universe exists only because of me and I am its controller. I am the only one who resides in each and every creature here.' Thus, it is impossible to realize Him merely through physics.

Astronomers have recently discovered a huge star, the largest to date. Named VY Canis Majoris (Red Hyper Giant), its diameter is approximately 2,80,000,000 miles. It is so huge that it would take 1,100 years at a speed of 900 km/hr, to orbit it. There are crores of stars and planets in our galaxy alone, and astronomers deduce there are 100 billion galaxies in the universe. Indeed, even today's rockets, satellites or future photon rockets would fail to determine the expanse of such an unbounded world.

So how can we know this boundless universe? Some philosophers believe that the speed of the mind is greater than anything else, and that it can traverse billions of galaxies in the fraction of a second. In order to know about this world and its creation, our mind need to make certain assumptions. As in mathematics, an assumption like 'suppose a = c' is necessary for further calculations, but in reality this 'suppose' does not exist. Then what should be the 'supposition' our minds should hold in order to realise the truth about the universe?

Our brain or intellect needs data in order to learn something. It sends messages to the mind by cross-verifying the information provided by the organs, along with stored information. It relates the rope to a snake only when it has stored the knowledge about the rope and comes to the conclusion that a snake is like a rope. It would fail to do so if the brain was oblivious about a rope or anything resembling it. Considering this, what could be the basis for discovering and learning about the creation of the universe? What assumption would the intellect seek to realise the Almighty? Just the travelling of the mind will not suffice; the intellect has its limitations.

An intellectual atheist would say, 'I believe only in that which appeals to my intellect and that which my eyes can see. I do not believe in God's existence as I cannot see Him'. This highlights the fact that only those things exist which the organs can see or feel. However, it may be surprising to know that what the organs can see or feel, may or may not actually exist in reality. For example, a dog's eyes see only in black and white and butterflies see the world in pixels. Since this world seems different to different creatures, which is the real world? Is the real world only the one which humans see and experience?

Even if it were so, the perception of the world differs from person to person. The world of dreams is also distinct from the real world. Incidents in a dream are seen and felt exactly as in our real world. We emerge from the joy or sorrow of dreamed experiences only when we awake, into a state of *awareness*. But can the possibility that our state of awareness is a prolonged dream, be ruled out? Illusion feels like reality because of our sensory organs. This means that all the things we experience may not exist in reality; it is just the mind that keeps creating patterns or meanings from what the organs experience.

In the last century, the British philosopher, John Locke, put forth this opinion: 'That which man acquires knowledge is the outcome of the senses of external things. The mind just 'reacts' or 'responds' to it.' This was modified by the famous German philosopher, Immanuel Kant: 'The mind does not simply respond or react, it also actively participates in the phenomenon'.

Today, scientists know exactly how the human brain forms an image within a fraction of a second. When we see a car, the light or rays are reflected from the car to our eyes and an image is formed on the retina. The photo-sensitive cells in the retina discharge electrons. In this process, the electro-chemical impulses get activated and travel to the visual cortex in the brain, through the optic nerves. The information thus gathered goes through complex processing about the car's shape, type, color and speed. The brain then integrates the information into a coherent whole, creating its own reconstruction of the external object and the brain recognizes the object as a car.

Similar to what we 'see' is what we 'hear'. In the case of a *sitar* player, the striking of the strings creates pressure waves in the air which stimulate the minute hairs present in the ear, sending electrical impulses to the brain, which analyses the information received from the ear. Our mind then gets the 'feel' of listening to the *sitar*.

Many such examples can be given, such as the smell of a mango. Its fragrance is sent to the brain, which then allows us to 'feel' it. The mind's response to all our senses is active. As already seen, the brain sends the received information to the mind by analysing it on the basis of stored information.

Here, the process of passing on information obtained in a state of awareness to our mind through the brain, is logical. However, it is difficult to understand the things seen in dreams. If we say a *dream* is not a state of *awareness*, then how can one 'see' things in it? What is the process of forming and sending images which we do not see in a state of awareness, to the brain? How is it that we can 'feel' them? What is the driving force of all actions such as hearing, running, eating, etc. in our dreams? The answer can be obtained only from a blend of psychology and philosophy. The impressions of our past lives and the experiences of our current life, are stored in our subconscious, and the mix of the two give us the experiences of the dream world.

To sum up: believing our eyes and our experiences, and depending upon them, is a relative concept. What we see is incomplete. We can see 4,30,000 to 7,50,000 gigahertz light, X-rays or Infra-red with our eyes. Similarly, there are limitations to all our other senses. Thus, all external phenomena might differ in their form, from those that we actually experience.

'That which *is* there cannot be *seen* and that which is *seen* is not like *that*' – this is known as *maya* or illusion by the

Indian philosophers. *Maya* does not mean *false* but a *delusion.* Shankaracharya, who advocated duality but experienced the divine union, expresses it as *Brahma Satya Jagan-mithya.... Chidananda Roopah Shivoham Shivoham.* It reinstates the principle that the Almighty is the only truth in this world. He expresses his illusion as, 'I am not the mind, the intellect, or the ego; all my organs are not 'me'; I am not the five elements, blood, essence, nor the bones, nor the five sensory organs. There is neither longing nor any expectations; no sins or otherwise, no joy or grief, no religion, philosophy, neither any sufferings nor enjoyment. Neither is there fear of death, nor am I stuck in relationships like the *Guru-shishya* or any relatives. I am unfathomable. I have no definite form...' Shankaracharya also said: 'I am the one who pervades the whole universe. I am the blend of all. I am Shiva which is nothing but the divine principle.'

When *yogis* experience such divine union, the world, along with their self, has no value for them, becoming *unreal.* This does not, however, prove that the physical world becomes illusory. Such an experience is possible when someone is asleep and the physical world around him becomes unreal for him. Two lovers on a bus, engrossed in each other, are completely unaware of the hustle-bustle around them, but this does not mean the physical world around them is illusion.

To test the water of the ocean it is not necessary to test the whole ocean; just a drop suffices to arrive at a conclusion. If each person can realise this principle resides within them, there would be no need to seek it in the outer world.

Yet, the question of how to realise this principle remains. According to the *Bhagavad-Gita,* 'Yog is the key to knowledge'. Yog here does not mean *yoga* as we define it today, it means 'to join, to unite'; it is the union of the soul and the Divine Principle – *Shiva Tatva.* To bring about this union, ancient

Indian sages had developed some techniques. But today, both the techniques as well as the deep thought behind them have been lost. The sages introduced idol worship so the common people could experience a state of bliss and divinity. The erudite pioneer of *Swadhyay*, Pandurang Shastri Athavle, presented the lost science of idol worship from a new perspective: everyone can experience the ultimate truth by following his own perception.

11. DEITIES

Two things are clear from the available data thus far – that the Gods may have been extraterrestrial humans or advanced creatures, who may have attained divinity; and that known and unknown powers in nature were considered to be Gods. *Suktas*, rhymes and *shlokas* were composed in reverence.

The word *Deva* possesses qualitative implications as well. *Dev* means 'amusement'. The qualities of the *Devas* or Gods were: those who found excitement in amusement, had consistency in order to triumph, were practical, possessed good qualities, had beauty, loved all, were grand, noble and sublime, surpassed pain and sorrow, had attained happiness, who dreamt of evolution, took pride in their culture and ancestry, always desired the welfare and wellbeing of others, and whose life was dynamic. These were the qualities of Gods which were worshipped in ancient times.

Several deities existed among the human race, who had different idols to worship. The Western countries too, have regarded deities like the 'God of love', 'God of sound', 'God of light', and the 'God of physical reality'. In ancient Greece, it was the practise to worship a pantheon of Gods. Alexander the Great was regarded as the son of God Zeus. Gods were being accepted by relation, experience or tradition. Gods emerged when humans became intensely aware of their own incompleteness and helplessness. The Gods had those magnificent qualities which Man wished to imbibe. The ancient human also surrendered before the overpoweing five elements of nature – wind, thunder, earthquake, lightning and rain. He invoked the Gods, pleading for mercy and compassion.

Religion and philosophy originated much later and became a three-pronged formula – God, religion and philosophy. The belief grew that there was certainly another hidden, unknown and fanciful world of Gods, beyond the living or non-living materialistic world.

In the *Rig-Veda*, Heaven or *Vishnu-lok*, is considered to be the Gods' abode. The perception is that the Gods in Heaven consume *somaras* and spend their life blissfully. The *Rig* and *Atharva Vedas* acknowledge 33 deities in all. Of these, 11 are considered to reside in Heaven, 11 on Earth, and the rest in water bodies. Taking a contrary view, Bhaskaracharya states that a single deity has presence in different worlds in different forms.

Dyauh, in the *Rig-Veda*, is the deity of space (one of the four elements). *Dyawa-pruthivi* (Earth), achieved the status of Mother and Father. Varun, the deity of the waters, is the most ancient and important deity of the *Rig-Veda*. Mitra was from the same era, hence *Mitra-Varun* came into use. Other deities like Surya, Savita, Pusha, Vivaswaan, Adityagana, Usha and Ashvi, were also revered in those times. However, Varun enjoyed a special status. Later, the Aryans instated God Indra, due to which the importance of Varun declined and Indra became the King of the Gods. Indra then became the national God for Vedic Indians. Later, Vishnu, who had risen to eminence, was considered fourth in significance. The legend that Vishnu encompassed the three worlds in three steps, finds mention in the *Rig-Veda*. Though dawn (*usha*), is a natural occurrence, it appears in the poetic form as *Usha-sukta* in the *Rig-Veda*. Similarly, Ashvinikumar, the twin Gods, who are never parted. They are the luminous Gods.

Deities like Indra, Trita, Aptya, Apaam Napaat, Maatarishwaa, Aja Ekapaada, Rudra, Marudgana and Parjanya, were regarded as Gods of Space. Indra was the God of War as well. All these deities, though sanctioned with various powers, were mortal. According to the ancient books, the Gods were never immortal. This seems to align to the Gods having been extraterrestrials.

The question remains: If the Gods were worshipped for their unparalleld virtues, how did they become mortals? Their mortality is mentioned even in *Shathapath Brahman* and *Aitareya Brahman*. In *Taiteriya Samhita* it says that the Gods had overcome death through celibacy, ascetic practice and *yoga-vidya*. Mythology says the Gods die at the end of each era. This can be accepted. Just as humans cease to exist, it is logical that the Gods, so regarded by humans as superior beings, ceased to exist too.

What of the mystery of 33 crore Hindu Gods? Over time, the term 33 crore (*koti*) gained several meanings and 33 crores is qualitative, not quantitative. The word *koti* here does not mean 'crore'; it denotes the quality of a virtuous (*koti*) person. The 33 crore Gods were all masters in their own fields – specialists. Surprisingly, the names of all the 33 *koti* Gods are known even today: Dhaata, Mitra, Aryamaa, Shakra, Varun, Ansha, Bhaga, Vivaswaan, Pushaa, Savita, Twashta and Vasu were the 12 Sun Gods. Dhara, Dhruva, Soma, Aha, Anil, Anal, Pratyusha and Prabhaas were the eight Earth Gods; Hara, Bahuroop, Tryambak, Aparajit, Vrushakapi, Shambhu, Kapardi, Reivat, Mrugavyaadh, Sharva and Kapaali were the fearsome 11, and then there were the 2 Ashwinikumars of the Sky.

With this background, the Saankhya system of philosophy seems quite different and advanced. It is an accepted fact that the pioneer of the Saankhya system of philosophy, Kapil Muni was the first to write the Yoga-Darshan and Patanjali Muni formulated it. Saankhya philosophy implies Dnyana

Marg, the path of knowledge. They are not atheists but they have a very different approach altogether.

Saankhya states that the Almighty is not immortal and that every creature who has attained realization is a ruler of the era. Saankhyas are of the opinion that the Almighty does not have any existence; they even assert there cannot be any single being as God. If it were so, the Almighty would have either a bound or a liberated soul. If bound, he would be trammelled by the rules of nature. How can he who is bound create the world? If his soul was liberated, why did he feel the need to create the world and organise it? Why would one who is self-contained feel the need to create a world?

Swami Vivekananda, while explaining the *sutras* (formulae) of Patanjali in the *Raja Yoga*, elucidates: 'Consider God to be the authority that manages or organises one of the facets of the world. Such divinity is availed of by several in rotation.' This explanation may convey the message that the Saankhyas are atheists, but this is not true – they acknowledge the Almighty to be an action-oriented Creator. Since Saankhya philosophy is based on the presumption that the doer is not required in the path of action (according to the principle of *karma*), they neither accepted nor opposed the Almighty. They believe Him to be an unconscious constituent, *Prakruti*, and a conscious being, *Chetan Purusha*, who is constant (permanent), all-pervading, intimate and comprehensive. After the *Vedas* and *Upanishads*, Saankhya philosophy, started by the highly intellectual Kapil Muni, may have died out with the passage of time. But the philosophy available to us today still exhibits the high intellectual caliber of the ancient Saankhyas.

On one hand, the noble ideas of Saankhya gained acceptance in society while on the other hand, deities from the *Rig-Veda* in the ancient era, embodied manifestations of virtue and prowess *sagunakaars*, which implies human form. This drew humans closer to the embodied forms. There was a vast difference in the deities based on nature, in the ancient era, and the human forms of the *Rig-Vedic* age.

Yama, the God of Death, was not considered so in the *Rig-Veda*. But Yama in mythology is the controller of Hell, looked upon as a destroyer, a retaliator and one who doles out suffering according to one's deeds. At first, Lord Ganesha was the God of creating impediments, but then he became the God who removed obstacles from one's path. Goddess Paarvati was Goddess Kali at times, and Annapurna, the Goddess of Food as well. Gods such as Brahma, Vishnu and Mahesh gained eminence. Brahma was labelled by the conservatives as not worthy of worship. This led to such a rise in the eminence of Vishnu and Mahesh, that they formed two major belief systems in India and gradually *Bhakti Marga* (path of devotion), became the accepted creed. These three deities had wives. Although Brahma was considered unworthy of worship, his wife, Saraswati, was the revered Goddess of Learning and the Arts. Lakshmi, the Doddess of Wealth was Vishnu's wife and the Mother Goddess, Paarvati, Shiva's consort.

There is a clear resemblance between the Summerian King, Akkadian (left) and Lord Ganesha (right).

Thus, several deities emerged in the Indian continent. People worshipped the deity who appealed to them. The cobra, the peacock, as well as demons, attained divinity too. The sages accepted all the deities of the Aryans as well as the non-Aryans.

However, during the mid-Upanishadic era, the interpretation of Gods became more intricate, yet universal. The gist of all the *Upanishads* is that all the vital energy centred within the human body, as well as in the universe, corresponds to divinity. The composers of the *Upanishads* categorised several powers that drive the cycle of nature as an organising, illuminating and working force. It encompassed the organization, growth and nurturing of the living and non-living world. The entire cosmos is filled with a vital motivational force – *pranashakti*, which is demonstrated through the deities Sun, Moon, Indra and Rudra. Breath is the God of Light. The *Upanishads* regard the body, mind, organs, intellect and life as 'soul'. All activities in this world depend on this spiritual power.

There is a fine blend of the *Vedas* and *Upanishads* in the *Bhagavad-Gita*; hence it is regarded as a balanced philosophy. The Lord instructs his disciples: 'You can worship any deity. I will strengthen your faith in that deity. You might even fulfill your wishes through his worship. But you will not gain *Me*.'

The *Bhagavad-Gita* advocates that to attain Him, one must pray with a devoted heart, a mind free of doubt, and an alert intellect. According to scholars, the *Bhagavad-Gita* was advocated in 3,101 B.C. or 5,600 B.C. In those times, man was on the path of falsehood, there was an upsurge of futile rituals, and religion and devotion had lost their meaning. The *Bhagavad-Gita* proved to be a guide then, even as it is today.

Noble personalities of ancient times were considered divine. Initially, they were revered for their virtues; gradually they became deities like Rama, Krishna, Hanuman, Durga, Mahadev. They began exercising their power over society. Rama and Krishna gained a special place in the hearts of the Hindus. Rama was favoured because of his qualities of monogamy, truthfulness and righteous conduct. Lord Krishna, mentor of the *Bhagavad-Gita*, was much loved for his multifaceted personality, diplomacy and political genius; he punished the corrupt. He was honoured variously as Venkatesh, Jagannath and Pandurang.

The depth of a devotee's devotion has a role to play in the peace and comfort he derives. Even if the meaning of *mantras* or *shlokas* are unknown, its benefits the devotee because of the intensity of faith and sentiment he brings in reciting it. A pure and intense heart displays a blissful state of mind. He reads a religious book or recites hymns like the *Hanuman Chaalisa* or *Wadwanal stotra*. They protect the devotee from harm. Regular recitations of such hymns strengthen the mind and help it to think righteously. The disciple benefits from it. Idol worship with a scientific approach gives the devotee a superior experience.

Rev. Pandurang Shastri Athavle has explained the science of idol worship in his book, *Scientific Idol Worship (Shaastriya Murtipuja)*. An idol is necessary for concentration or meditating upon. The idol should have a human shape and possess virtues, be expressive, and exhibit beauty of thought. With regular and sincere meditation, the image of the idol disappears and this gives the follower the experience of completeness. He unites with the Supreme Power and realises his own self. That is the purpose of idol worship. It helps the devotee transform his state of conscious meditation into a blissful state of mind. With regular practice, the mind becomes powerful, sensitive and progressive.

Thus, in this way, man derived happiness from activities like meditation and idol worship and attained peace. He began reaping the fruits of his deep faith in the Supreme Power, by leaving his worries in the hands of his preferred deities.

But this path of devotion, *Bhakti Marga*, began losing its sincerity. Idol worship and devotion slowly lost their original focus and became merely ritual. God, the Principle, remained only in name, to invoke during times of distress. The thought of attaining to the Principle by utilizing this human birth, was undermined. The urge to reach Gods and hence the self, declined. As a result, humans became engrossed in the outer materialistic world. This was taken advantage of by so-called *Gurus*. Spirituality became a business, a profession, and monasteries with the best facilities flourished. The belief that a *Guru* is the only one who knows all the answers was systematically and deliberately inculcated. This led disciples into adopting methods of worship to please their *Gurus*.

It says in the *Bhagavad-Gita* that emotion and trust with intellect means unique devotion – *ananya bhakti*; emotions and trust without the intellect means blind devotion – *andha bhakti*. Hence, an effort has to be made to reach the origin, the source, the core. The purity of the Ganges can best be experienced not at Allahabad, but at Gangotri, where it originates. Thus, each one has to strive to know the secrets of the Gods and of this world. Man will thus become more honest and virtuous and his mind will be diverted from materialism and discontent. The Earth and nature will flourish.

Swami Vivekananda said: 'Nature is eager to unveil all its secrets to you. There would be nothing left to acquire after having known about it.' The desire and effort to attain that knowledge is all that is required.

12. SCIENCE AND SPIRITUALITY

Swami Chakradhar cited the parable of an elephant in the context of God. Four blind people touched an elephant – the one who touched the tail said the elephant was like a broom; the one who touched its ears, said it was like a sifting fan; the third touched the elephant's stomach and said it is like a wall; the fourth touched a leg and said it was a pole. How could four blind people know the elephant in its entirety? Swami Chakradhar explains that knowing God is similar to this – only a sighted person can see the elephant in its entirety.

Yukteshwar Mahashay, *Guru* of Yogananda said: 'God's form is very simple, yet very complex. God becomes easy to realise only if there is true devotion in our life.'

According to Dr. Raymond Moody's research, life after death is timeless. It is human birth that gives life the feeling of being time-bound. Human life is just like a dream. Death is followed by stages, showing that there is a miniscule yet effective principle at the core of the visible world, which controls it. There is an *awakening* when a human being dies. Just like man is in a dream-like state in his sleep, man's whole life with all the events and happenings is like a dream.

We enter the dream world in our sleep. We may fall down, get angry, hate, feel joyful, fly in the air, build a house, travel or get tired in our dreams. While *living* these dreams, our sensory organs are active and we feel the pain of departure or someone's death, the joy of love. We can experience sexual pleasure and smell the fragrance of flowers. In brief, all our senses are satisfied in our dreams just as when we are awake. Humans thus experience their dreams. They meet dead relatives and friends; touch, sight, smell, taste and sound can all be experienced in dreams.

However, this dreamland disappears as soon as one awakens and becomes aware of reality. One realises that whatever one saw was not reality, it was just an illusion. In the same way, this world, comprising of nature, mankind and all its phenomena, is like a dream, practically experienced. Sri Sankaracharya said: '*Brahma Satyam Jaganmithyaa,*' meaning that it isn't that no events take place in this materialistic world, but that they die out. And so they are deceptive. The *Bhagavad-Gita* explains that because the world is bound by time, it is mortal and hence deceptive, like an illusion.

The renowned psychoanalyst, Dr. Sigmund Freud, put forth some revolutionary theories on dreams, sex and the functioning of the human mind. A human being has two minds – a small portion, one eighth, is responsible for his behavior and interactions with the outer world, this is the 'conscious mind'. He is ignorant of the larger, seven-eighth part, which is the 'unconscious mind'. Further, Dr. Freud presented the theory that the unconscious mind stores man's lust and desires. Fear of society or a virtuous atmosphere, suppresses these desires, which get accumulated in the unconscious mind and lead to emotional and health problems. If these desires are fulfilled, their negative influence gets dissipated.

The whole world was shaken by Freud's theory that the fulfilment of desires was the key to a happy life. His theory was accepted by the Western world, where a devastated family system has resulted. However, according to Indian philosophers, the mind is a temple. Gaudpadacharya suggested the mind cannot be divided merely into two parts, the conscious and the unconscious, but that it has four categories – the first being the *conscious mind*, the second the *sub-conscious mind*, the third the *unconscious mind*, and the fourth the *super-conscious mind*. This is also known as *Turiya*. The sub-conscious mind is active while in the dream state. Dreams are realised from the experiences stored in the unconscious mind, along with images and experiences noted by the conscious mind. Often, we see things in our dreams which we have never seen or imagined before. This is perhaps possible because some elements from the unconscious mind have entered the dream. When the mind, which creates consciousness, comes under the control of a devotee, he can perform inscrutable tasks such as knowing the thoughts of another person, or about the past and future. These relate to the materialistic world. Thus the real image of God cannot be realised from this and we need to travel further in order to enter His domain. This is a journey of the senses, mind, intellect and beyond, to the inner self or the soul. This journey is known as the path of spirituality. Spirituality means the search for the Almighty, the science behind the search for the Creator of this world. Having an intense desire to realise Him and adopting a method to do so, is the path of spirituality.

Today, scientists also are trying to discover more about the world and its creator. Therefore, can we consider such scientists spiritual too? In spirituality, the mind, senses, intellect and ego need constant nurturing. Scientists, while doing their job, may not be living such a nurtured life, hence, though the goal is the same, they cannot be considered spiritual. Scientists use materialistic tools while spiritual people use the mind. Western philosophers do not perceive the mind as a separate entity, and that everything concerning the mind happens in the brain. Thoughts are generated in the brain and end there too. This theory implies that after death, the mind dies as well. However, the fact that the mind exists even after death left Dr. Raymond Moody astounded.

Those who are deeply acquainted with the *Shastras*, believe it is the mind and not the brain that has a separate identity. This is the basic difference in the approach of philosophers and scientists, though their objective is the same. Both attempt to go beyond the dream state and discover the truth. To do this, philosophers condition the mind with specific virtues and then try to reach the inner self. They attempt to identify the immortal principle by achieving real awakening through meditation. Scientiests utilise the resources in dreams to explore the elements external to the dream state. Their search becomes endless. All their efforts remain restricted to dreams, and end there.

The awakening man experiences after death makes him aware of actual reality as well as what is but dreams.

God can only be known through the path of spirituality. Now the question arises as to what exactly has to be done to follow such a path? Does spirituality mean following the typical rituals like worshipping God, chanting His name, counting beads, and fasting? Does man thus become spiritual? The first thing is to change one's mentality. Practising rituals does help, but that it is not enough to make one spiritual. One must also possess devotion towards God. Rev. Pandurang Shastri Athavle asserted that devotion is not an act but a state of mind. *Bhakti* (devotion) is the basis of understanding. The Almighty has enabled man with skills and virtues to practise devotion. Work can become an act of devotion when done with all one's heart, and God as witness. Thus, Rev. Pandurang Shastri says: 'God eats when we eat, God puts in effort along with us when we work, and when we sleep, God does not sleep but protects us by staying awake.' Anyone can begin the spiritual journey by using this approach.

In today's world, there is a huge gap between spirituality and day-to-day life. Science stresses researched elements, whereas religion assigns importance to values. Science thinks in terms of true or false, religion in terms of good and evil. Science anticipates man's materialistic advancement, while religion desires man's spiritual (inner self) progression along with materialistic (external self) advancement. The solution for many problems could be found if science and spirituality worked in harmony. It is necessary to reduce the gap in order for society to become prosperous in the true sense. Materialistic society must understand spirituality, and vice-versa, so that spirituality becomes equally prevalent. This would eliminate narrow-mindedness. All of society must have a common aspiration towards God. All human cannot become ascetics. So, *Swami* Ramdas asks us to follow our duty in our worldly life. The fine association between spirituality and materialism is the major factor in the creation of an ideal society.

How can comprehensiveness be brought about in spirituality? Let us consider the following points:

1. An egotistical mentality must gradually die out. Merely reading spiritual books or reciting verses from them can never make anyone spiritual. The *Bhagavad-Gita* says that such obsessed bookworms are good-for-nothings. Nobody should carry a false pride in their virtues or achievements.

2. God has instilled certain qualities in each individual and we should appreciate them. For instance, a construction worker possesses certain skills, a farmer toils in order to grow crops, a carpenter has the ability to make furniture, and a poet or writer has the talent to communicate. Each individual is unique. Although people are professionals in various disciplines, they

can have devotion to the Almighty through dedicated work. Each one earns his livelihood depending on his skills and intellect. Instead of being envious, one should extend appreciation and encouragement. Therein lies our greatness – by appreciating others we appreciate God. Valuing everyone in the world is divinity. We must learn to respect it. The saying, 'Appreciate others, then others will appreciate you' must become part of people's very nature.

3. People must give up a self-centred attitude and get involved in others' lives, be sensitive to their struggles. One has to emerge from his cocoon of '*my* world, *my* ego, *my* family and *my* needs'. Rev. Athavle thus suggested the practice of selfless work – *nishkam karma yoga*, by introducing *bhaktipheri* and *bhaavpheri*, making them self-learners. There are many who struggle with their own problems, yet work selflessly for others. Thousands practise *karma yoga* and carry out the task of inculcating good values in the population, while giving due consideration to their emotions and beliefs. Even people lacking moral values are given due respect. This is social service, devotion and morality in its truest sense. Seven centuries ago, Saint Dnyaneshwar formed the Varkari Sampradaay, a community whose sole purpose was such work. Sant Tukaram, Sant Namdeo, Sant Eknath, among others, adopted the same path.

4. It is equally important that while being spiritual and philosophical, we do not to discredit science. Each field has its importance. Criticising materialism and deliberately living a miserable life with no creature comforts, and then approaching a doctor during an

ailment, is clearly a defective way of looking at things. It is important to value scientists, who also attempt to unfold the secrets of the world.

If all humans support each another, this mortal world would become easy to understand and experience. On a spiritual level, humans would feel more enlightened. The following story of the hare and the tortoise throws light on this:

Once there lived a hare and a tortoise. They decided to have a race. The first to reach the tree on the hilltop would be the winner. The race began. The hare obviously quickly ran ahead while the tortoise moved at his slow crawl. Seeing the tortoise lagging far behind, the hare stopped for a nap. In the meanwhile, the tortoise, plodding upwards, overtook the hare and made its way to the tree on the hilltop at a slow and steady pace. The hare awoke and saw the tortoise wasn't behind him anymore, but sitting under the tree. He felt ashamed that despite his natural speed, he had lost the race to a slow creature like a tortoise!

This is the version of the fable that we've heard in childhood. But a new version of this story is equally important:

The defeated hare did some quick thinking. 'I'm a champion in running. Yet, how did I lose against a slow-moving tortoise?' Upon reflection, he realised he had lost because of his overconfidence and laziness. So he challenged the tortoise to another race. The tortoise, filled with pride at his victory, agreed to the hare's proposal without a moment's hesitation. The race began. But this time, the hare won and the tortoise lost.

Now it was time for the tortoise to do some introspection. He realised the hare could run faster on land, whereas he could swim faster in water. Thrilled by this knowledge, the tortoise approached the hare and suggested a third race, saying, 'Let us race once again, but not on this hill, for I am tired. We will race on flat land."

The hare flushed with pride and immediately agreed.

The tortoise said, 'Look, there's a plateau over there...'

'Yes...'

'There is a stream beyond it...'

'That's true.' The hare's self-confidence rose.

'There is some flat land further on and then a pond...'

'Yes okay...'

'After crossing the pond, there is a river bank...and...'

'That's fine. I agree," said the hare.

Once again the race began. The hare ran at top speed on land and then stopped, whereas the tortoise went ahead in the water. He trundled along and crossed the stream, pond and river with ease. The tortoise easily won the race. The hare realised the trick played by the tortoise and began thinking again, but he could not think of a way to beat the tortoise. God has conferred upon each creature some abilities and some weaknesses, the hare realised.

The hare said to the tortoise, 'We both have some skills and some weaknesses. But there is one way in which we can overcome our flaws.'

'What is that?' asked the tortoise.

'Through team work. Let us have a final race. I will carry you on my back while running on land, and you will carry me in the water. Do you agree?"

The tortoise agreed and they began this final 'race', which wasn't really a race but a journey of mutual understanding.

If jealousy and envy were to be replaced with healthy competition and mutual understanding, society would progress. Cooperation and companionship would make people more sensitive towards each other's sorrow and happiness. People can empower each other and gain lasting satisfaction and happiness through team work and mutual understanding. Cultivation of such positive values in society can solve many problems. When a major part of society is happy and content, only then will people be drawn to the Creator. Science and spirituality together can transform society.

13. THE CONSCIOUSNESS OF BEING

Swami Ramdas narrates in *Dasbodh*: 'A soul, while in its mother's womb, says "*Soham*, I Am That"; and "*Koham*, Who am I?", on entering this materialistic world.'

'What is my existence about in this disorderly world? I am so worthless, my thoughts so shallow. Yet, depending on my inadequate knowledge, I try to understand the world. I have an intense urge to know the world in its entirety. But I also challenge the existence of the Creator.' Such thoughts are contradicted by positive thoughts like, 'In this vast world, I have a minuscule existence but I am a tiny part of the spirit and life on Earth. I feel my existence only because of this spirit. I owe my virtues to this power and I feel honored.'

Throughout his life, a human being keeps searching for the answer to 'Who am I?' Holy men, who had experienced this path of knowledge and devotion, have opined that 'I Am' (*Soham, Aham Brahmasmi*), is the ultimate realisation. A part of the Almighty resides within us in the form of *Pratyagama*, a fraction of the super soul.

But how can a person engrossed in the material world realise *Soham* if he is unable to experience it? If he could do so, it would definitely bring about a great transformation. A layman may say, 'Who can tell what happens to us after we die? Why should we ruin the present thinking about death? Who knows whether there is a Heaven? Enjoy the present, that is all.'

There is a tendency among social reformers to deny the existence of the Supreme Power. Many people proudly state that they don't believe in God. This class of society, who uproot the Divine Principle, has gained respect too. However, trying to inculcate spiritual values through education is a difficult task since today's education system focuses on materialistic development. The Western approach emphasises better education to enable future financial gain. But student are not taught to think about self-development and self-realisation. Society is stuck in the duel between individuality and totality. Self-development has become a negligible part of man's life.

In this context, let us look at the following example. There is a story in the *Chhandogya Upanishad*, about Satyakaam Jaabaal. He approaches a *Guru* to gain knowledge. The *Guru* asks him his name, place of birth and details of his ancestors. Satyakaam adds, 'Acharya-ji, I am unaware of my ancestry, since my mother is a servant and a prostitute. But even she does not know who my father is... I am not rich, but I follow the path of righteousness. I speak only the truth. My behavior is impeccable. Will you still be my *Guru* and impart knowledge to me?' The Acharya said, 'Satyakaam, you are the right student to gain knowledge from me because you are honest and virtuous.'

When the British ruled India, Lord Macaulay weeded out the ancient Gurukul system of education. Generation after generation became materialistic. There began a race to imitate Western culture. Development acquired a new meaning – affluence, competition, greed for material things, creating unnecessary needs and desires, and living beyond one's means. The Government built a network of roads and railways, huge dams for water storage and to generate electricity; it set up security and defence. All this required heavy expenditure. Corrption became rampant and morality degenerated. Beautiful towns became chaotic. People became reckless.

They were caught in a vicious cycle and became restless, discontented and unhappy. The basic notion of happiness changed as people began to behave in an unethical manner; a debauched lifestyle seeming attractive and prestigious. People had the means, but no inner peace. They became agitated.

Kaalo wa kaaranam Raadnyaa Raja wa kaalakaaranam | Iti te sanshayo maabhoot Raajaa kaalasya kaaranam || This ancient principle states that a King is not created by a situation, rather, the King himself creates the situation, reaping its fruits accordingly. In this frantic era, every responsible parent attempts to provide the best education to their child so that he can stand on his own feet when the time comes. But money cannot wipe out the restlessness the child feels because he hasn't had a *real* education which will help him achieve total bliss. His education is devoid of truth, non-violence, piety and righteousness. 'When education is imparted, virtuousness gets absorbed,' is a maxim which is no longer true.

A mother proudly tells her neighbour, 'My younger son is very smart and can take care of himself. He is shrewd and I need not worry about him. But I'm worried about the older one. He is straightforward, gullible and virtuous.' How degenerative this is. We are unfortunately victims of the times. During ancient times, a virtuous Satyakaam proved to be a meritorious candidate for education. Even though he did not belong to any caste or creed he was given due respect. But in today's world, it is the shrewd and selfish person who gains respect. So the mother is concerned not about the selfish one but the one who is naïve and gullible.

The time has come for each of us to assess our adopted path. Most of us want to achieve peace but the path we choose may not be apt. People seek solitude, but being alone does not bring peace. They surrender to gurus but later realise those 'holy' men are not holy but opportunists. People engage in meaningless rituals and bothersome events, and possess a grudging devotion. Most people worship God with the aim to fulfilling their desires. This is just a reflection of reality.

The *Bhagavad-Gita* states, that apathy towards God is the major hindrance in attaining Him. But how can He be realized? If He cannot be attained despite a lifetime's effort, any human being would be right to question God's existence. Witnessing God or feeling His existence is not an easy task. In the *Bhagavad-Gita*, the Almighty says: 'Out of a thousand beings, just a single being endeavours to realise my true essence; and only one in those thousands truly understands me in essence.'

Why not be one of the lucky few? But what exactly is meant by making efforts to achieve Him? How can we achieve God in the given circumstances? Swami Vivekananda asked Ramakrishna Paramhansa: 'Have you really seen God?' and Ramakrishna replied: 'Do you still have any doubt, Narendra? I have seen God as I am seeing you now.' Highly spiritual men like Ramakrishna and Vivekananda and Sant Dnyaneshwar have experienced the *Tatvamasi* (I Am That) principle, but what can the common man do to achieve Him? Is he even capable of following in the footsteps of such great men? The *Bhagavad-Gita* says that merely following religion does not take us any closer to achieving Him. Meditation, a state of trance, requires great concentration of mind. Arjuna says to Sri Krishna: 'O Krishna, it is easier to win over the three worlds than make our minds stable with just one thought.'

Yogi Yogananda once went to meet Gandha baba, the 'perfume saint', who could manifest any aroma with his yogic skills. This left people entranced. Gandha baba said to Yogananda: 'A 12 year long meditation practice helped me acquire this skill.' Yogananda asked him: 'But did you experience God during this period?' 'I did not,' was the reply. But Yogananda did not believe Gandha baba had not seen God in 12 long years of meditation. He mentioned a Persian visionary, Abu, who laughed at people who performed miraculous acts, saying: 'A fog is also at home in the waters. The crow and the vulture easily fly in the air. The Devil is concurrently present in the East and in the West. A true man is he who dwells in the righteous among his fellowmen, who may buy and sell, yet is never for a single instant forgetful of God.'

In short, though miraculous acts like walking on water or flying in the sky are accomplished, they do not indicate God realisation. Meditation brings about several benefits like peace of mind, vigour, brilliance, and radiance, but not God's realisation.

So in what way can ordinary people witness God's existence? There is one way – we can get a faint idea of God's existence if we try to understand what happens to us after death. Man has long tried to understand life after death. There are references to life after death in the dialogues between Nachiketa and Yama, in the *Garud Purana*. There is also much discussion on the topic in the *Bhagavad-Gita*.

Let us familiarise ourselves with recent research on death. Death is a frightful word. The poet Govind, who asserted: 'I will grow beautiful, I will live by death,' is an exceptional human. But we ordinary mortals do fear death. The venerable Pandurang Shastri Athavle said: 'Death is not so horrifying; it is beautiful. Rebirth is inevitable. God loves nature very much. He has offered man free will.' This means man can attain his own prosperity. He can do it for others as well. He can beautify the natural world too, since God has given him free will. He could begin to perform virtuous acts if he got a glimpse of death. His free will would be channelized, his *Karma*

Yoga (path of action) initiated. He would then understand the meaning of life and the futility of self-centredness.

To glimpse death does not necessitate us to experience death. Our secret travel through this territory in the following pages, will be based on the findings and thoughts of all those who have made a systematic and scientific effort to understand, and then put forth theories about life after death.

*****

PART III
ACHIEVING THE SUPREME POWER

14. UNIVERSALITY OF THE MIND

Hypnotherapists use a technique to help us know about our past lives. The subject is taken back in time, through hypnotism. Gradually, during this process, his childhood memories are revived and then he goes into a previous lifetime. He can then describe his past life, his birth place, people and events, in great detail. It is difficult to know whether he thus becomes aware of his past-life memories, which are forgotten in his current lifetime. It is for each of us to choose to believe or not.

But we can try out the technique ourselves with a different approach. First, we need to go back in time to birth, then we can think of our existence prior to our current lifetime, and ask questions such as: Who was I before this birth? Where was I?

'I' (*Aham*) will exist till this world exists. 'I' remains the same at every stage of childhood, youth and old age. The existence of 'I' neither diminishes nor increases; similarly it never gets weary. 'I' was there without the mortal body and will be there after death. This means there is actually no relation between the body and the principle that resides in it. The principle, *Aham*, may have resided in some other body in a previous birth, but for how long? Perhaps in inumerable bodies over aeons of time. Human history is believed to date back four lakh years. Scientists are of the opinion that this world was created millions of years ago, which raises the question: What was the existence of 'I' before the world began? Was 'I' existent? These thoughts mesmerize and astound the mind.

At the same time, we should consider that our present birth is of less than 100 years duration for most people. Will 'I' exist after abandoning this body? The answer is: Yes. Since 'I' existed prior to this birth, it will exist after this birth as well. But 'I' cannot escape the joys and sorrows of each birth. For how long will 'I' exist? Will there be reincarnation on Earth or on one of the planets in space, in a new body form? How many such rebirths will 'I' take; how long will 'I' go through this cycle of birth, death and rebirth – for millions of years or until the end of this world? And when the world ends, will 'I' still exist? All these thoughts are spine-chilling.

Along with this, we can also ponder over other aspects such as today 'I' am bound by this body and restricted. My human vision cannot encompass the entire world. Many solar systems are situated at great distances of light years from Earth. Within the 100 or so years of my lifespan, I definitely cannot see this colossal world. Whatever is hidden is indescribable and amazing. Though I lack the ability to reach it, I still wish to know it. But is it possible?

I, the person, am engrossed in a world of my own – myself, my home, my family, my status, my money, my selfishness, unable to funtion beyond eating, shopping, customs, festivals, enjoyment, lust, etc. I find joy in all this. Therefore, I am oblivious to the ultimate happiness that is hidden in this beautiful world.

But we can be drawn to the path of meditation and contemplation. Mediation (a state of absence of thought), can be practised early in the morning or at night, when the hustle and bustle of the world around us ends. The word 'meditation' is also commonly used to mean concentration, but, in fact, it has a wider meaning – a prolonged state of concentration. One has to practice pushing away the thoughts that clutter the mind and focus on 'I am not confined to this body'; I can see the sky from Earth; I am looking at the solar system and this galaxy and all of it is being absorbed in my eyes; this galaxy is clearly visible to my eyes, the entire world is there in front of me.

In fact, it is not the galaxy that has become tiny but that I have grown bigger. It is my vision that is encompassing the world. Only if we look at the world through this vision, can the mind attain universality. We then become conscious of the power hidden within us which broadens our vision. This develops purity of mind, guiding us further to the achievement of ultimate happiness. Our journey from materialistic gains to personal happiness begins.

The cause and effect theory of the Almighty is incomprehensible. For example, clay is the cause of a pot, and the pot is the effect of the clay. This means the form of the clay can be deduced once the form of the pot is known. Ice is the effect of water. The form of water can be guessed when the form of ice is known. Cause and effect are inter-related. However, this theory does not apply to God. The known (manifested) world, has God's existence in the background. This world is the effect, and the cause behind it is God. However, God cannot be known by knowing the world. This means that God is incomprehensible through the study of the elements present in the universe. Scientists, researchers, sages and philosophers have all tried to realise Him over thousands of years.

God-realisation is the ultimate goal of human life. But can the common man attain it? It is difficult, but certainly not impossible. The goal is unattainable through materialistic means, for it is beyond the mortal body, time and the intellect. The human body is both time-bound and form-bound. It is like searching for a movie star in the cinema hall while the movie is being shown. We thus have no option but to keep trying to gain this knowledge by going beyond time. Here, we obviously turn to *Yoga Shastra*. Five thousand years ago, the sage Patanjali Muni systematically presented *Yoga-Darshan*. He maintained that control over all the senses (organs) and deep meditation, was indispensable for attaining knowledge.

It is difficult for the common man today to find time for all this in the fast pace of modern life. Those who can, benefit from *pranayama*, *yamaniyam* and *yoga*. However, it does not lead to the attainment of knowledge, it provides sound physical health. A strong urge to gain knowledge is equally important, as is purity of mind. Sins accumulated over time, the good and bad *karma* of our past lives, needs to be cleared. Only then can one begin this journey towards knowledge. Purification of the mind changes the form of *Aham*. The otherwise restricted *Aham* is transformed into a universal and broad frame, changing the nature of a human being, and leading to purity in his thoughts and deeds.

It thus requires us to raise our level of sincerity and virtuousness. It is difficult for a common man stuck within the restrictions of family, children, work, household, etc., to suddenly gain the support of *Yoga-Shastra*, nonetheless, he can definitely nurture good values by practicing *yoga* and *karma yoga* – the right path of action. We can thus raise our level of virtuousness by using those tools conferred upon us by nature and God.

The main tool is the mind. But man's intellect has its limitations and cannot overcome its built-in boundaries. But the mind does not have any limitations. It has unimaginable speed. We can break all ties linking us to our past lives with the help of the mind. We can even manifest our desires. On waking, say a prayer and affirm (with the mind), that: 'Today will be a better day for me than yesterday; I will do more good today; I am of sound health, my body is healthy and free from any disease [if already ailing: I am getting better); my body is healthy, strong and tough as steel.'

Similarly, at bedtime, instruct the mind: 'Forgive me, God, for any wrongs that I may have committed today; tomorrow I will work better.' The Almighty expects we will try to fulfill our promise of good conduct and thus acquire His love. Such affirmations and prayers bring positivity into our lives and nurture our mind with virtuousness. *Rajasi* (lustful) and *tamasi* (ignorant, hot-tempered) behaviour, gets curbed.

Human beings have three qualities: *Satva* (morality), *Rajas* (lust) and *Tamas* (ignorance). We see the effects of the dominant quality in each individual. Usually, the effects of a combination of two qualities are seen.

There are numerous problems all around us. Incidents like murder, rape, accidents, pollution and depletion of our natural resources, corruption and lust for power, are the effects of a distorted attitude of mind. Some people attempt to institute measures to maintain a degree of normalcy in society. However, it is a frustrating exercise, like trying to patch up the innumerable holes in a ship's bottom.

The intensification of the *Rajasi* and *Tamasi* qualities leads to anarchy. All measures to bring want and greed under control, prove inadequate. Materialistic people dominate. As a result, a selfish attitude keeps the whole community dissatisfied. In this way, one day man will completely destroy nature, just like a worm completely consumes a leaf. The only solution to this dire scenario is to foster virtuousness.

15. THE LAW OF KARMA

Indian philosophy believes in seven worlds. Apart from this, the Masters have put forth theories of rebirth and the law of *karma* (actions). It has also been mentioned that those who have attained the highest spiritual level, are able to recall all their previous births. Lord Krishna discusses this with Arjuna. This profound philosophy was broadly outlined in the *Bhagavad-Gita* 5000 years ago. Scholars say the *Gita* was uttered at the battle of Kurukshetra, in 3101 B.C. Three paths – action, knowledge and devotion – have been recommended for the attainment of salvation.

The *Bhagavad-Gita* is a different topic of contemplation altogether, forming a fine association between rebirth and deeds *(karma)*. Our deeds, good or bad, form bonds. We attain higher levels as the bonds of our deeds are released. Suffering for our bad *karma* is inevitable in this birth or in a subsequent birth. Rewards for good *karma* also follow us. Rebirth for our good or bad *karma* is inevitable, there is no escaping it. Man remembers God in times of suffering, but he enjoys a pleasurable life because of the good *karmas* of his past life, and here he gets trapped. All the theories related to God, divinity, *karma*, are ignored during his period of prosperity. As Marathi litterateur, N.C. Kelkar, said, "The prosperous period is the period of sins." Man loses his self-control because of the success he achieves and this leads him onto the path of sin and vice, taking him back to square one.

It is unlikely anybody can reach the higher plane in such a manner. The higher plane is more advanced than this materialistic world. The ancient masters, when asked about the path that can lead us to the ultimate, final plane, have advised us to follow the path of good *karma* or selfless work. These *karmas* or deeds are mentioned in detail in the *Bhagavad-Gita*. Only we can become our own saviours. The Masters also mention the theory of *Aham Brahmasi* in the *Upanishads*: 'We are beyond, life and death, beyond space and beyond time. We are God, and they are us.' A quote by Pierre Teilhard de Chardin, says: 'We are not human having a spiritual experience; we are spiritual beings having a human experience.'

The *Gita* tells us about the three-fold aspect. In 14th chapter, the three qualities, *Satva*, *Rajas* and *Tamas*, are explained in their entirety. Man carries all these three qualities within him. Each quality shows its effect according to its intensity, just like the three phases of a day – morning, afternoon and evening are expressed differently in a single day, in the same place. These qualities are gifts from God. *Tamasi*, the ignorant, hot tempered quality, leads to materialism, depletion of natural resources, unemployment, violence, cut-throat competition, etc. However *Satva guna* is superior to the others. In order to bring about positive change in society, *Satva guna* is the quality to be practised in our day-to-day lives. This can be done if we, as a society, stop chasing the gitterati and follow the path of our philosophers. Today, *Rajas* and *Tamas* are in full force. The downfall of civilization is the sure outcome. Let us consider these qualities, as given in the *Bhagavad-Gita* before discussing *Satva guna*.

Rajoguna: The person with this quality enjoys external pleasures. He easily gets swayed by external attractions but the initial pleasure is followed by pain. He is never satisfied, always in a wanting state. His devotion is self-centered. His love is not for God but for His favours. He takes undue advantage of religion for material gains. The traits of such a person are agitation, ritual worship, lust, restlessness, etc. His favorite tastes are bitter, sour, spicy etc. Such persons enjoy grand marriage ceremonies, huge parties, birthday celebrations, etc. (in today's context), to portray themselves as religious and superior. They give alms for the sake of gaining popularity ('wannabe' personalities). *Rajasi* people are of the opinion that the soul is different in different individuals, so they look at God differently. The knowledge possessed by *Rajasi* people is dual vision. Such people are constantly seeking to fulfill their desires. They rejoice when they succeed but are distressed when they fail. Material gain gives them pleasure, like nectar, but ultimately it leads them to sorrow and pain, like poison.

Tamoguna: This quality emerges from ignorance. It makes a person insane and forgetful of his duties. He becomes lax. He is far from gaining knowledge of his self. He takes pride in his ignorance. His actions and thinking become sluggish. His sensory organs remain quite active but are not synchronised with his actions. He desires gain without pain, and is ever ready to take the wrong path to gain his objectives. Imprudence, blundering, neglect of one's duties, succumbing to temptation, are some results. Persons with this quality have a preference for half-cooked, dried, foul-smelling and preserved foods. People with *Tamoguni* traits harm their own body and soul, with the intension of hurting others. If they become ascetics, it is through the wrong path. Their understanding of asceticism means renouncing one's duties, leaving the family, and leading a wandering life. They believe the body to be the soul and take pride in assuming the body to be the whole. They do not have any true knowledge of it, and are ignorant of the repercussions of their actions in dealing with power and money. They are oblivious of the trouble they cause to others, including animals. A *Tamoguni* person is always restless, ignorant and unenlightened, yet full of false pride and cunning. He feels pride in destroying others' means of subsistence, yet always suffers distress. He is stricken with fear, grief, melancholy and lust. He is lost in the pleasures of sleep, laziness and blundering.

Rajoguna and *Tamoguna* together result in errors. These qualities tend to rise together or in turns, and accordingly affect the social system. Presently, we are going through the phase where *Rajoguna* and *Tamoguna* have risen – *Kaliyug*. In this context, it would be prudent to consider the characteristics of *Satvaguna*, as outlined in the *Bhagavad-Gita*.

Satvaguni: A virtuous person is like the pure and immaculate morning light. He constantly strives to attain God instead of getting engrossed in his created pleasures. This clear-as-crystal quality can be developed as he becomes selfless. He never causes problems to others. Such a person is aware of *Aham* and so he stresses the need for pure happiness. He achieves a perfect balance of mind and intellect, and hones his sensory organs. *Satva guna* gets elevated whenever conscience gains knowledge and happiness. As *satviks* (virtuous persons who worship God with pure devotion), they have perfect control over themselves. Such human beings, who sincerely strive to attain God, gain the desired knowledge and a state of bliss thereafter. They enjoy fresh, nutritious food which makes them strong, increases their lifespan and nurtures their mental health. They devote themselves to the highest power without any expectations. Therefore, such persons do not get carried away with success, nor do they become miserable in failure. Their deeds are pure and free from lust and greed or other negative emotions. They have perfect control over their thoughts through the practice of *yoga*. Control over the organs, concentration, a state of meditation, a state of trance, are hard to achieve in the initial stages. However, *satvik* people are ultimately successful in achieving all this and in finding true bliss.

In short, man strives for happiness but his efforts prove futile if done aimlessly. Such efforts only cause misery. Therefore, boosting of *Satvaguna* is of prime importance today, and it is possible only through a disciplined approach. If the profound philosophy of the *Bhagavad-Gita* can be absorbed into our lives, it can lead all of mankind to peace and prosperity.

Today, there is unrest and distress everywhere. The rich and the poor are both miserable. Any solution to this seems superficial. The ultimate solution is the rise of *Satvaguna* (morality), which is possible by following the law of *Karma*, thereby inculcating purity of thought and conduct, thus inviting peace into our lives.

16. CELEBRATION OF DEATH

The word 'celebration' is usually used for happy occasions. In the context of death, it may appear offensive. Although death is agonising for the bereaved, it is a blissful state for the dying. The following explanation will make this statement clear.

We all fear death. It is considered an unpleasant event. The thought of it creates all kinds of doubts in our minds, such as letting go of everything we have worked so hard to achieve. The mind is cluttered with questions: Where will I go after death? Will I exist after death? Will I become a ghost or spirit? It would be nice if I went to Heaven, but what if I go to Hell? How will my family deal with my absence? I have to leave everything so what was the point of struggling so much? This reminds us of the freedom fighters like Veer Savarkar who used to say, 'I spent each day of my life engaged in doing good deeds. I did not waste a single day. So I would be free from worry at the twilight of my life.'

We should definitely strive to engage in performing virtuous acts, each day of our lives, more so if we have glimpsed death. But what is the unknown territory of death like? The American scientist, Dr. Raymond Moody, has systematically studied the subject and written a beautiful book, *Life after Life*, which became a bestseller when it was published in 1975. Moody taught philosophy in North Carolina University before pursuing medicine. He continued his studies in psychology as well. He was especially interested in studying death.

A few years later, Moody did a systematic study and wrote his book. He specifically mentions in the preface, that his work is not based on first-hand information, but on the near-death experiences of other people. He kept his research and findings confidential and travelled extensively to meet such people, persuading them to share their experiences. He analysed the data in a scientific manner. He then segregated the information on the basis of the period of time people remained in that state. Moody put down his unbiased observations. There were, surprisingly, great similarities in the death experiences.

The Death Experience: What is death like? Sasha, brother of Vladimir Lenin, died in childhood. As his soul left his body, he suddenly shouted, 'What's that?' What was it that he saw? What does a human being see when leaving the body? What does he experience? Hundreds of researchers have worked on this subject and many people have had near-death experiences. The findngs are summarised below.

1. Some people hear the sounds of bells at the time of death.

2. They experience speeding through a dark tunnel or space.

3. The spirit or soul moves out of the body through the head. Nearby, a presence urges us to leave the body. It calls us. (Could it be the one always present in the body as *sakshi*, witness?)

4. Some hear divine, melodious music never heard on Earth.

5. The soul floats to some distance above the earthly body and looks down at his dead body from there. If he has died in hospital, he sees the nurses hurrying about, the doctors trying to revive him.

6. Once out of the body, the person realises certain things when he sees his body from above. He can now see

without his eyes, hear without his ears. Not only this, he can also read the minds of the people around his dead body. He is able to watch people, hear them speak and read their minds. His own thoughts form at tremendous speed. When the doctors and nurses take him to the ICU for instance, he accompanies them in his floating state. While moving through the air at great speed, he easily passes through solid objects. He can hear people speak but the others cannot hear him when he tries to tell them something. He is conscious of his existence. He is aware of the fact that his spiritual body is of the same size as his earthly one, or it is circular, made up of plasma matter. He also realises he does not have any organs but possesses extra-sensory knowledge.

7. The mind experiences a delightful state after parting from the body – extreme happiness, never felt before. He acquires knowledge of his soul.

8. After leaving the body, he sees a radiant image form. It is bright and luminescent. Such radiance cannot be witnessed on Earth. He stares mesmerised at this pure light. Though it is so powerful, it does not harm the eyes of the 'dead' one. On the contrary, he feels enveloped in its warmth and enjoys a state of immense happiness.

9. The presence of this aura is very pleasing and it makes him fearless. He has a feeling of contentment. In our ignorance, we keep making mistakes, committing sins, blaming others for our petty mistakes and holding onto grudges – because of anger, jealousy, ego, and intolerance of others' faults. But the aura showers this human bundle of blunders with pure love. This figure of light 'talks' to

the 'dead', without words; communication takes place through the transmission of thoughts. Such a mode of communication seems strange and surprises the 'dead' person. It also means that whatever we think and do when we are alive, is stored somewhere. We have to face the consequences of that, for good or bad. Thus our minds need to attain purity.

10. The figure of light caringly asks, 'Are you willing to come? Cross this line and then you will know.' The 'dead' person knows about the line but he is unable to see it. This is a time of bliss; he has attained a state of ecstasy. The figure then says, 'Let us take a look how you lived your life.' The question comes from one who knows everything, yet is loving. The 'dead' person's life flashes like a slideshow at great speed. Strangely, though he sees his whole life flash by in seconds, he is able to recollect everything with great clarity. In short, his mental capacity increases tremendously. While 'watching', he reexperiences his childhood. Also, he can 'see' how he has wronged others. He realises the things left undone.

This flashback is beyond our current understanding since it is neither a film nor a slide-show. All the incidents witnessed are illusions for the dead. Some scenes are visible in three-dimension, and moving, while others are in colour. The 'dead' person can actually see himself breaking a toy in his childhood. He watches all this as if recorded by somebody else. But who? Is it the *sakshi* (witness), as we refer to it? The radiant figure does not study the life of the 'dead' person but tries to teach him something.

Thus, the 'dead' one learns that birth and death is a continuous process. We are here with a mission, to perform virtuous acts.

Each one is bound by duty to show others the path of gaining knowledge. We cannot change our past. In life after death, there is no place for regrets about deeds done while alive, we must go through another birth to correct our misdeeds. Spiritual science says that each one has to bear the fruits of our deeds, good or bad, in Heaven or in Hell. It is beyond anyone's capacity to change it except by taking another human birth.

Soham (I am, the spiritual being), takes another birth to nullify earlier misdeeds and to perform virtuous acts. But once again, on taking birth, he utters *Koham* (Who am I?). The memory of his previous birth is limited. He is stuck in ignorant oblivion, and starts to err once again. This series of births and deaths thus continues. Sant Dasganu writes in *Gajanan Vijay*, that it is obligatory to take a new birth in order to undergo sufferings for past life deeds. Then how many births are needed?

According to the ancient sages, the *Vedas* and the *Bhagavad-Gita*, human being appears before Chitragupta first when he dies. (Is the divine figure who records one's life, Chitragupta? Are these records known as *Akashik*?) He looks at the *karmic* balance of a man's good and bad deeds.

Some people have also experienced death's latter stages. We will consider that later. It is important to know about the knowledge gained by people who experienced death but survived. The recorded experiences of such people are more or less similar. The general opinion is that: 'The death experience is unique and transcendental. It made all our fears disappear. It is strange that people fear death. It was an incomparable, joyous experience. It is impossible to have such an experience on Earth. The 'light' seen at the time of death can never be seen while living.'

The 'dead' person becomes conscious of his past deeds after the death experience. He realizes he has been rude to others, oblivious of his wife's pain and efforts, and must now perform good deeds and fulfill his duties towards his family and society. The most important thing he realises about life is that this human birth is for doing selfless work, for gaining knowledge and making others knowledgeable.

The *Bhagavad-Gita* gives us the same advice. The importance of selfless work is explained rationally and convincingly. The *Bhagavad-Gita* tells us about the continuous cycle of birth and death. A human being takes with him after death, his deeds, just like the breeze bears fragrance. The final *karmic* balance (of deeds) becomes *nil* only through selfless work and by gaining spiritual knowledge. However, a man loses his past memory the moment he takes a new birth. Thus begins a new game of ignorance. He challenges His existence and begins a new series of misdeeds which are either *Rajasi* (lustful) or *Taamasi* (ignorant, hot-tempered).

Swami Vivekananda said this is a game of God. It is up to each individual to decide how long he wishes to play this game of distress. If we follow the path of *nishkam karma* or selfless action, our past memory can be revived. People who have achieved this elevation, step by step – *Suchinam Shrimantam Gehe*, meaning they take rebirth in excellent families, conducive to spiritual growth, and finally achieve salvation. Salvation or liberation is a state of eternal bliss. Selfless deeds any time in life can nullify the previous *karmic* imbalance. Man can liberate himself when he regains the memory of his past lives, about his existence, his origin, his life after death, and the purpose behind his birth.

Thus, towards the end of the *Bhagavad-Gita*, Arjuna says: *Nashto Moha: Smrutirlabdha,* when he regains the memory of his past life and mission in Chapter 18. He becomes aware of the task entrusted to him. If we, the common people, were to become aware like Arjuna, what a great transformation there would be in society!

The Later Stages of Death: The 'dead', after communicating with the luminous figure, have a few more experiences to relate. They are mentioned verbatim as follows:

1. *A boundary line could be seen in front of me. A grey light like that of fog could also be seen. I could also witness the body attempting to take shape with water.*

2. *I could see something like a beautiful farm. There was a greenish light spread all over. A golden light, not yellow light, was also seen by me. I have never seen such light on Earth.*

3. *There was a compound or a boundary line ahead. I started going towards it. There was a hazy human figure standing on the other side. It approached the compound to welcome me.*

4. *I could spot an ocean-like water body extending to the horizon. I could feel I was sailing to the other side, sailing through bhavasagar. I could see my deceased relatives waiting to greet me on the other side. All these scenes appeared to be superimposed.*

5. *It was misty and I could see human-like figures beyond the fog. It was so blissful to walk through the mist that the joy cannot be expressed in human language.*

6. *All of a sudden, I saw my dead uncle on the shore. He said, 'Go back, your mission on Earth is not yet accomplished'.*

All these anecdotes help us conclude that the death experience is quite extraordinary. It is a blissful state that we cannot achieve on Earth. All those who went through the experience received immense, pure love from the figure of light. The deceased relatives were also aware of the deeds and incomplete tasks of the 'dead' one. The human figures were hazy and indistinct.

There were green hued, farm-like scenes, or a boundary line, and someone present, waiting to welcome them.

Western research on life after death has served to substantiate the ancient Indian texts. But it is up to each individual to believe these findings or not. However, death experience-realisations act as a catalyst for the performance of good and virtuous deeds, which benefits society as a whole. For personal and social evolution, following the wisdom of the *Bhagavad-Gita* is always beneficial. Once we gain knowledge of the soul, life becomes the performance of work, selflessly.

17. RISE OF VIRTUOUSNESS

The Almighty has endowed all creatures with more or less similar emotions but human beings are the greatest creations of God. He is blessed with long-term memory, unlike most animals. Humans are considered to be the wisest of all living creatures since he possesses many more skills and abilities than other creatures. The ability to think, create, use his hands, as well as complex emotions like pity, love, forgiveness and compassion are naturally present in him. Any creature so advanced, is blessed with positive qualities. But there is a stage beyond human physicality in this universe. It is only in striving to this level that humans gain virtuousness.

Lack of honesty and righteousness are the major factors responsible for the undesirable state of society today. But they can be righted by practising concentration, self-control, charity, appropriate diet, deep sleep, etc. But as the founder of *Swadhyay*, Pandurang Shastri Athavle, states in *Kenopanishad*, today there is speed in our lives, but there is no living.

Nonetheless, we must find time from our frantic schedules to nurture virtuousness and fuel our whole being with this quality. We can make proper use of our abilities in the following ways:

Sight (vision/attitude): We can train our eyes to *see* beauty, not in a lustful manner but from a pious and emotional viewpoint. It is regrettable that TV serials depicting wrong values such as family disputes, violence and unethical behavior, are regularly watched in every household and are preferred topics of discussion.

Every action creates an imprint on the sub-conscious mind. The 'hard disk' in the human brain, if crowded with negative thoughts, is the cause of innumerable problems. Instead, we can train ourselves to *see* only the good and beautiful things, abundantly present in our universe. Today, we hardly look up at the open sky. Each of us should take the time to watch the sky with its infinity of stars and planets. It is worth filling our minds with wonder and asking: How do stars or planets float like this for billions of years? Who created them? What is my existence in the universe for?

Natural phenomenon such as rivers, lakes, various types of birds and their intricate nests, waterfalls, mountain peaks, trees, the infinite sky with its changing colours, flowers, the grass swaying in the wind, sheep, clouds, fill our hearts with delight. Like nature, there are many other things that give us joy – art forms, musical instruments, a perfectly directed movie, and so on. But not everybody notices. Most people are oblivious to the happiness and joy they bring. Only when we absorb and enjoy the offerings of man's skill, can we make them a part of our own happiness. The pleasure hidden in bountiful nature can be unveiled only when we stop looking and start seeing. It is thus critical to develop 'vision'.

Hearing (listening): Our minds must be trained to attract good thoughts, our ears habituated to listening to the music created by *pandits, ustads* and *supremos* who have dedicated their talents to mastering a skill. Today, amateurs performing on television attract undeserving attention, as viewers have limited knowledge. Hence, cultivating an ear for supreme music is essential.

Speech (words): There is some power within us that witnesses our speech as we utter words and our thoughts as they arise in our minds. We realize this only after reaching the highest level of virtuousness. First, our thoughts surface in the mind, after which we put them into words, our organs working together to do so. This process would not happen if a single organ was non-functional. A child learns to speak by observing the lip movements and gestures of others. He is not taught the technique behind speaking a specific word, the grammar or syntax. Yet the child learns to speak effortlessly.

In fact, there is a Power which is the driving force behind all things, however minor or insignificant they may seem. That power or designer, we call 'God'. It should be borne in mind that whenever 'I' speak, it is actually the Power speaking through me. Hence I should not speak ill, nor offend or hurt anyone, since God speaks through me. This is called *Vachik tapa*, or verbal penance. Pandu, in the *Mahabharata*, had taken a vow not to speak ill of anyone, to avoid foul language and prevent evil thoughts emerging in his mind. Such a vow helps to purifying our speech. By doing so, we become *Satvaguni* or virtuous beings.

Action (acts and deeds): Once human nature becomes pious, bad deeds are avoided. However, improving our *satvik* quality requires perfect control over all our faculties. The mind has to be trained not to hurt anybody, but to help society. Purity of thought, word and deed then leads to our ultimate happiness.

A ball thrown into the air, returns to the ground. Similarly, thoughts generated in the cosmos by the mind, come back to us. Evil thoughts bounce back, as do good thoughts. To rebound is the law of nature. The timing of the rebound is, however, not known. It might happen immediately, or after a span, or perhaps in our next birth. The memory of past evil deeds and thoughts lie forgotten, hence a person remains confused about his virtuousness and his suffering in his current birth. Regardless of whether we regain the memory of our past, like Arjuna, or not, practising good conduct is a worthwhile endeavour. Our actions or thoughts are constantly noticed by a built-in Power. Just being aware of this will improve our patterns of thoughts and deeds.

Diet (food): Diet does not mean just consuming food, but fulfilling the needs of all our organs. The *Bhagavad-Gita* advocates diet control and emphasises a controlled lifestyle. That is why it is necessary to keep a check on one's diet and a *satvik* diet is recommended. A non-vegetarian diet increases the quality of *Tamas* (ignorance, hot temper). Ultimately, this quality leads man to destruction. It is essential to control one's diet in order to curb the *Tamasi* quality, as the type of food eaten directly affects disposition. The consumption of alcohol, meats, deep fried or spicy foods, etc., is harmful.

The thought that alcoholic drinks or meaty foods at parties or get-togethers is harmful, does not normally cross our minds. The justification is often that the occasion demands it. But such excuses are feeble. Following the rules of diet is imperative to avoid degeneration of both body and mind. Eating meals while watching television is also not recommended, since the emotions being shown on screen directly affect the food being consumed, and the negative energy is deposited in the body, sure to create problems.

Love of Nature: Man does not value nature. Emgrossed in his manmade world, he tends to disregard it completely. But the world is enslaved by time, for we are mortal. Instead of seeking superficial happiness in passing, we must endeavour to attain ultimate joy. All scriptures and philosophical books guide us down this path.

Do not ignore nature while practicing penance. Rather, experience the bountiful and beautiful world around us with our God-given faculties. If a man starts his penance with negative emotions such as hate, how can he love God with a selfless heart? Therefore, he should first learn to love His creation. He will be dumbstruck by His vision, and the system that controls this visible, tangible world. Such thoughts draw us closer to Him.

Our curiosity increases and the mind fills with thoughts like: How did God infuse aroma and colour into flowers? How did He set laws for nature? How did He schedule time? How did He make the stars shine? How did He instill talent in man? Pondering over such questions gradually increases our devotion to God.

Perception of Talent: Overall awareness not only gives the *saadhak* (seeker), the experience of competence within the universe, but he also becomes aware of the talent latent in every human being. Virtuousness takes shape. It diverts man from materialistic desires to soul satisfaction. His journey towards self-realisation begins with the help of man-made tools. However, it is necessary to understand any kind of aptitude. God has empowered each individual with some skills and talents, which must be respected. Some people have a personality that is enriched from within by penance, devotion, virtuous deeds of past lives, etc. God resides in such people and their talent has reached the heights of perfection. Deference for such people and such talent, and feeling oneness with them, is the same as loving God.

Conditioning the Mind: Where is our mind located? Is it in the heart or brain? Wherever it may be, we can feel its existence. Sigmund Freud was of the opinion that we have two minds –internal and external. The external mind is the one we use normally. We utilise just an eighth of the mind, what we know; the remaining seven-eighths is unknown to us. Past lives' impressions and memories are associated with this part of the mind, which comes along with us as data, in our current lives.

Consider the computer and internet. When we log in, there are temporary files. C-drive gets affected if a virus enters the computer but it does not affect D-drive. In short, C-drive is exposed to the outer world (internet), and we can email, chat, read information, use social media, send and receive photos, listen to music, and gain knowledge on various topics. Similarly, our external mind finds pleasure in this world. It can think and express love or hate; we live with its support.

However, man is unaware of the most powerful, seven-eighth part of his mind. Knowledge of the universe is stored there. Data about past lives, impressions, penance (*tapa*), study, etc., are all stored, just like the data on a computer's hard disk. It is never wiped out, but comes as an add-on with each new birth. This is all science. All the data of our past lives is loaded in our current birth. This is known as *karmabandha*. This continues till we are released from the karmic cycle and the data is finally erased and the soul freed.

It is possible to free ourselves from the cycle of fate and experience ultimate happiness, in our current birth. It requires us to erase the data stored in the powerful, unexpressed, rewritable mind. How can this be done? By reaching that final level of virtuousness, and for that, we need to introspect. Once our attitude towards the Creator changes, it automatically draws us toward penance. The belief that God resides within us grows stronger. We can also form associations with people who have similar beliefs. Get-togethers with a selfless attitude, celebrating festivals together, arranging potluck dinners, organising seminars to discuss culture, civilisation, poetry, science, etc. can all be done. These activities discourage self-centredness.

The mind becomes stress-free and blissful. A mind focussed on happy thoughts transmits positive vibrations.

18. DIVINE RESONANCE

The eminent vocalist, Pandit Manhar Barve, used to say there is sound everywhere. Indeed, there is music everywhere. Pandit Barve produced melodious sounds from a wooden instrument, but he also created sweet notes using a saw-like tool. Every particle of matter on Earth sends out expressed and unexpressed sounds. The bubbling of streams, the rushing of a flowing river, the roaring of breakers on the shore, fascinate everyone. Ustad Bade Gulam Ali Khan often did his riyaz (vocal exercises), near the ocean. His notes would vary with the variations of the waves.

Music that is in harmony with nature is supreme. Wind, when it swishes through a dense forest, makes a rushing sound. The hide of a dead animal, when stretched, also makes a sound. There are innumerable activities going on inside the human body, without a break, creating continuous sound within the body. Even the Sun and the Earth make continuous sounds while rotating. This is called *Anahat dhwani* or 'unbeaten sound'. It is not easily audible in today's busy world with its distractions and noise pollution. Perhaps such a sound is created by our bodies as well. But who is listening? The 'final destination' (God), can be reached if we can capture this sound. In other words, this sound takes us to our ultimate destination, for when we hear it we have reached the final level of introspection – from where one can progress from divine resonance to the final resonance.

Just like an idol aids a *saadhak* in his meditation, the chanting of *mantras* creates specific frequencies in the brain. Sounds help meditation. Many people try to enter the divine territory (God), by chanting *mantras* like *Aum* and *Bhramari* (humming in a specific rhythm, with precise pronunciation). The devotee's brain becomes charged with the rhythmic sound, as does his entire body; evil and negative thoughts are washed away. Practicing *Bhramari* consistently can give the *saadhak* a divine experience. There are many different *mantras*, chanting of which may be part of family tradition. *Mantras* like *Aum Gang Ganapataye Namaha, Aum Namah Shivaya, Aum Namo Bhagawate Vaasudevaya, Aum Tat Sat, Hari Aum*, etc. help to produce positive, refreshing energy and good vibrations, changing the overall atmosphere in the house. Breathing gets charged with these mantras and the vibrations get assimilated into the body.

Most devotees perhaps follow this path but this writing attempts to project a clearer picture of *Naada-Brahma* or divine resonance. Sound is capable of producing tremendous energy. However, not every type of sound helps to achieve peace of mind, satisfaction, positivity, etc. Music is always beautiful, irrespective of its origin. Our age, location and upbringing influences our taste in music. However, those who wish to create a positive, joyous, peaceful and divine atmosphere around them, and wish to reach the 'final destination', should listen to music of a specific type – *Shastriya* music. [The word 'classical' has been used for Indian *Shastriya* music in order to take readers closer to the meaning, but *Shastriya* doesn't mean classical.] Music from popular cinema may sound melodious, but it has restrictions. Light music is like a beautiful lake when compared to the vast ocean. One cannot be compared to the other. *Gaganam Gaganakaaram* – the ocean is incomparable.

Indian classical music has evolved from the penance of *rishis*, hymns, *suktas* from the *Saama-Veda*, etc. – it is a vast ocean.

Even by diving deeply into it, we cannot gauge its expanse. Light music is short-lived and soon forgotten. This is not the case with classical music, which has a prolonged effect. Its sounds remain with us even when we have finished listening. The slow rhythms keep buzzing in our minds and affect both body and mind positively. Recent studies show that music therapy can help in healing diseases. Just as Ayurveda is not a therapy for healing diseases, but a Veda used to build a fit and healthy body in order to facilitate the journey towards the ultimate truth, music too, is a supremely sweet medium not just for healing, but for realising Him. The prominent singer Kishori Amonkar has said, "Music is a penance, not a goal." To sing is not an achievement but a penance. We reach the ultimate goal through its help.

My mother, Sanjeevani Kher, is an eminent singer. She would tell us that if great singers invoked *Raga Maalakans* with deep intensity at midnight, the singer or player would actually see the Goddess. It is said the lamps in court would light up when the great singer, Tansen, sang *Raga Deep*. Some opera singers can shatter glass. Some seemingly incredible events have actually occurred. Pandit Manhar Barve once went to a famine-affected village in Uttar Pradesh to perform. When he sang *Raga Megha-malhar*, it began to rain. The point is that music has such tremendous power that it can bend the laws of nature. Our goal can be accomplished merely by listening, if singing does not come naturally to us.

What is the type of music best suited for our purpose and when should it be listened to? There are many *gharanas* (lineages) in Indian classical music – Kirana, Mewati, Jaipur, Banaras, Agra etc. There are variations in the elaboration of each *Raga* according to the *gharana*. It is for the individual to follow his choice.

The Path to Happiness through the Aural Medium: A baby in the womb is attuned to the various sounds it hears. The same happens after he is born – he tunes in to the world, judging things around him by touch and sound. Later, he gradually finds his bearings by using all his senses. As he grows up, he is entranced by material attractions and starts chasing these pleasures, considering them to be the truth of life. The more he yearns for such objects and experiences, the further he gets from his original state of bliss. If he wishes to return to the *Soham* state of real happiness, he has to divert himself. One tool is music. Just by listening to divine music, he is sure to experience joy beyond any materialistic happiness.

Music is not a goal but a medium for approaching the ultimate path. If we are unable to listen to music for a long time, due to our hectic schedules or lack of quiet time, our brain starts creating music inwardly. This is known as 'musical ear syndrome'. It is because music is the natural food of the brain. If deprived for a long time, it starts creating its own music.

We are aware of the positive effects of music on the brain. In today's world, life is difficult due to tough competition, hard work, busy schedules, insufficient time to relax and de-stress, resulting in a tired brain. To rejuvenate ourselves, we need to listen to music. If this hunger for music is not sated, the brain begins to create its own music and tries to de-stress itself.

Musical tastes differ from person to person, and range from the classical to popular, modern and devotional. To understand Indian classical and semi-classical music, one needs to listen to it over and over again. We need to prepare our minds to listen. To listen properly to classical music, we should hear different *Ragas* according to the time of day or night. This creates a pleasant atmosphere that becomes divine and pure, making the environment calm and serene.

An Indian artist once performed a morning *Raga* in front of a foreigner in the evening. He asked, 'How did you feel, listening to this?' The foreigner, a complete stranger to Indian classical music, replied, 'I felt as though the Sun was rising from behind the mountains, birds are moving towards the east; I felt like it is dawn.' That is the power of Indian classical music, which is based on *layakari*, the wavy effect or flow of *swaras* (notes). Western orchestral music, based on collective effect, exhibits its greatness by structuring different forms on various instruments being played simultaneously. This music too, is profound.

Modern music and songs, with their meaningless lyrics, composed for noisy parties, are high-pitched and ear-piercing. Such music is mechanical and artificial. A few years ago, an experiment was carried out in the US, at the Mahesh Yogi Center. Cancer cells were isolated and placed in two soundproof labs. In one lab, there was loud, shrill music being played, and in the other, Indian classical music. Both cell samples were tested after a specific length of time. It was observed that the cells exposed to cacophonic music had multiplied, whereas the cells where harmonious sounds had been played had simply vanished! Indian classical music is a proven tool in fighting disease. Soft, soothing music creates a restful environment in busy places like offices, hospitals, shops, banks, hotels, etc.

Popular music satisfies our senses as they relate to the material world, whereas Indian classical music illuminates the path of ultimate happiness. Since *layakari* is the basis of Indian classical music, it is deep and touches the heart. This music feels divine. The *Raga* is well-structured by the ancient masters and various *Ragas* continue from early morning to well past midnight. Performers create their own forms, based on their knowledge, understanding, devotion, experience and training. Western classical music has the same effect though the instrumentalist cannot make any changes in the musical structure.

Here is some information about the various *Ragas* that can be played at various times of the day. They help to create positivity, happiness, satisfaction, health and peace in our lives.

Early morning: *Lalat, Bairagi, Raamkali, Bhairav, Jait, Nata-Bhairav, Basant-bukhari*, etc.

Late morning: *Desi, Deshkar, Gujari Todi, Jaunpuri, Asavari, Miya ki Todi, Bhatiyaar*, etc.

Afternoon: *Bhimpalas, Saarang* and its types, *Multani, Madhuvanti, Gaavati*, etc.

Evening: *Bahaar, Basant, Puriya-Dhanashree, Maarwaa, Shree, Gauri, Puriya*, etc.

After dusk: *Yaman, Maarubihaag, Bihaag, Pancham, Bhinna shadja, Kafi, Raaj-kalyan*, etc.

Night: *Baageshree, Rageshree, Shankara, Kedar, Chaaya-nut, Bhoop, Shuddha-kalyan, Rajeshwari, Hansadhwani*, etc.

Late night: *Darbaari, Naayaki Kaanada, Suha, Kaushi-Kaanada, Durga, Malkans, Chandrakans, Jogkans, Jayjayvanti, Jog*, etc.

When it rains: *Malhar* and its types: *Miya-malhar, Megh-amalhar, Soor-malhar*, etc.

On a starry night: *Pahadi, (Raagini), Jhinzoti, Bageshree, Mishra-kalyan* and *Zula, Phagun, Hori, Chaiti* and *Daadara* are semi-classical *Ragas*, related to seasons and festivals as well.

To de-stress and for a peaceful mind: *Darbari, Jhinzoti, Bhoop, Shuddha-kalyan, Jog, Jayjayvanti, Kaushi Kanada*, etc.

Spiritual Experience through Music: In discussing the influence of the 7 *sanskaras*, the importance of 7 is phenomenal even in the laws of nature – there are seven seas, seven heavens, seven wonders of the world, seven births, seven Rishis, a week has seven days, and so on. Likewise, there are 7 primary colors, and 7 *swaras* (notes) in music. These notes form the basis of all music, in combination with the *shuddha* (pure) and *komal* (soft) flat notes or tones. There are innumerable compositions based on these 7 *swaras*. In Western music, these notes are called *Do Re, Mi, Fa, So, La, Ti* and their Indian equivalent is *Sa, Re, Ga, Ma, Pa, Dha, Ni*. The pitch of these notes has to be accurate and this is possible only through practice. *Shastriya sangeet, thumri, ghazal, kajari, zula, hori* and rhythmic Carnatic music, is good for regaining mental peace, healing disease and creating a peaceful ambience for self-realisation.

The intention here is to guide readers about deriving immense pleasure and happiness through divine resonance and a divine experience of musical notes or *swaras*. The joy one experiences varies according to the intensity of one's devotion and discipline. The experience of bliss is special and cannot be either completely objective or entirely subjective. Those who strongly aspire towards soul-realization, can achieve this blissful state through study and practice of the 7 *swaras*.

It is advisable to first accustom our ears to the glorious music created by eminent masters. I too, have experienced a state of bliss and been able to pull myself out of tough situations and illnesses by listening to such uplifting music. Both the *nirguna* (unmanifested) and *saguna* (manifested) forms of devotion are powerful. Meditation takes us from manifestation to spirituality, initially worshipping the manifested form and then attaining spirituality and union with the Almighty. It is the spiritual state which is achievable through music.

Music has aptly been referred to as *nirguna* (unmanifested). Philosophy, however, does not regard music as *nirguna*, since spirituality is a state of being in the manifested.

However, *nirguna* is a state in which qualities do not need to be expressed and the *swaras* create a state of trance. We can close our eyes and create another world with the help of universal music. Words do not exist, nor are they important. We can actively participate in the world we have created, or just remain a witness.

We are responsible for the change in lifestyle in order to focus on self-realisation. We have become addicted to mindless television serials and negative news. Thus, they who wish to attain ultimate happiness through music, must first make the effort to gradually change their lifestyle. The first step would be to have an early dinner and go to bed by 10:30 p.m. Those working night shifts need to find the best solution around their schedules. One can then easily set aside half an hour for listening to music. To experience a blissful state, one is required to follow some simple rules.

1. It is advisable to switch off the TV during meals. Watching movies and soap operas that highlight family disputes, extra-marital affairs, discord, immorality, violence, corruption, helplessness, etc. should be avoided.

2. Other than reading, do not engage in activities using electronic equipment after dinner.

3. Days are for working and nights for resting. This is nature's law. Sadly, many go against it. Nonetheless, those who can follow it, should make the effort to attain serenity through music and then enjoy sound sleep.

4. Schedule spiritual practice so as to maintain consistency and avoid any break in the routine.

5. Music can be enjoyed while seated or lying down.

6. The volume should be adjusted to be pleasant to the ears.

7. Dim the lights in order to focus on the music and not get distracted by visual stimulii.

8. Calm and soothing moonlight appears between the 12th of the month till the full moon. [Though witnessing this has become rare, it can be imagined with closed eyes.] Listen to following music according to the moon's phases:

Rising moon: *Ragas: Bihag, Marubihag, Yaman, Bhoop, Shudhha Kalyan, Shaanti-preranaa, Vachaspati, Pahhadi, etc.*

When the moon tilts towards the west: *Ragas: Jhinzoti, Kaushi kaanada, Chandrakans, Bhoopali, Bhoop, Bageshree, Malkauns, Rageshree, etc.*

The performance of the *Ragas Jhinzoti* and *Shaantiprerana* by Shivkumar Sharma, Hariprasad Chaurasiya and Bhavani Shankar (*Pakhwaaj*), have attained excellence in musical quality and their calming effect. These *Ragas* should be heard by a novice, and then enjoyed in depth.

Dark night: *Ragas: Darbari, Nanda, Bihag and Jayjayvanti, Jog, Nayki Kanada, Abhogi, etc.*

The above information is necessary to set aside the tensions of the day. Believing that God will solve all our problems, a deliberate effort must be made to separate ourselves. It is equally important to ponder our deeds, good or bad, at the end of each day, and so try to bring about a change in our everyday conduct.

What to Watch: While listening to music of this calibre, our inner eyes can view certain images taking shape according to the *Raga* or notes. This experience takes us towards pleasure-giving *saguna* (beauty). While listening to *Shaanti-prerana* or *Jhinzoti*, we can visualise beautiful scenes such as snow-laden mountain peaks that soothe the soul. One can even witness flamingoes wandering in Mansarovar, Mount Kailash in the background, and feel the intense purity of the place.

Mount Kailash

Mount Kailash is said to be the home of Lord Shiva.

While listening to *Hori*, *Kajari*, *Zula* or any other Pahadi composition, Lord Krishna can be seen dancing with the *gopikas* in Vrindavan We can thus deeply participate in this blissful experience, using this simple technique. Likewise, we can witness Lord Rama and his wife Sita, seated on a swing decorated with fragrant flowers, while listening to *Siya Sang jhule bagiya mein Rama...* and we can see Laxman giving the swing a slight push, while listening to '*Lakhana Jhulave...*'

Thus, we can invoke divine images which give us pleasure and happiness. With the consistent practice of such musical meditation, one day we will realise that the reason we can view such divine images is 'I'. Happiness lies within us. 'I' am a form of happiness. 'I' am the creator and the participant. Such manifestation can happen.

This is a journey of uniting with nature; with the universe and its Creator. On this path we lose the materialistic attitude and develop love and tolerance towards all living creatures. Universality takes the place of narrow-mindedness. This makes us feel lighter and more heart-centred; we feel His presence. At times, our heart overflows with emotion. We understand the meaning of life. Futile rituals and thirst for knowledge lose their importance. Questions such as: 'Who were the Gods?' 'Were they extra-terrestrials?' 'Does He exist?', or 'Did Rama and Laxman exist?', carry no meaning. Purity of soul is achieved and the journey begins from body-awareness to soul-realisation. Our mind, rather than our body, becomes healthy and free of illness. The state mentioned in the *Bhagavad-Gita* as *Nirmamo Nirahankaar, Maitra Karuna Evacha*, is experienced in its truest sense. Life unfolds its real meaning and a high level of spirituality is reached. This creates the yearning for self-realisation.

Whoever desires ultimate truth and happiness can endeavour to achieve it by following the path of penance.

19. SIMPLE METHODS OF MEDITATION

Five thousand years ago, Bhagwan Patanjali formulated the *Yoga-Shastra*. Today it is known as *Paatanjal Yoga-Darshan*. It explains in detail how *yoga* can be performed by exercising control over one's senses and organs, using techniques of *Dhyan dharana* (concentration), *Pratyahara* (withdrawal of the senses from external objects), and *Samadhi* (meditation). Please note, concentration does not mean meditation. Later, many other *yogis* followed this path and successfully adopted the yogic lifestyle. *Yog-marga* is also called *Siddha Yoga, Pantharaj, Shaktipaat Yoga, Pashupat Yoga* and *Kriya Yoga*.

In Bihar, the science of *yoga* is systematically taught at Yogavidya Dham. The great sage, Mahesh Yogi, has gone a step further and propagated TM (Transcendental Meditation). In the last century, Avtar Babaji's disciple, Lahiri Mahasaya, and then his great disciple, Yukteswar Giri, initiated *Kriya Yoga*. Yogi Yogananda, disciple of Yukteshwar Mahasaya, has widely propagated *Kriya Yoga* in the US. Some *sadhakas* (followers) follow the path of *Naam-saadhana*, (chanting of the name of God), to achieve meditation. All these methods lead to the same end – self-realization.

Those who do not wish to get involved in *Guruism* and its related rituals, yet wish to follow the path of self-realisation, have two options – the first is scientific idol worship and the other cosmic energy penance or *saadhana*. The *Bhagavad-Gita* tells us we can uplift ourselves. Anyone can do so by choosing one of these paths.

Path One: *Murtipooja* – **Scientific Idol Worship**
Ancient Indian sages have explained the science behind this simple method of meditation but it was forgotten over time. What remained were just routine, meaningless rituals. However, in this era, the pioneer of *Swadhyay*, Rev.Pandurang Shastri Athavle, has re-established the science of idol worship. Let us briefly review his explanation.

Murtipooja or idol worship is a unique doctrine in Hindu mysticism. Semitics around the world believed that such worshippers were orthodox aborigines. It was only when Nicholas of Cusa, in his book, *Vision of God* (1453), put forth his thoughts on icons that scholars finally understood the advanced views on idol worship held by the Hindus. Nicholas himself made several attempts to meditate on an impassive God, but in vain. Then, he began to follow an icon, and gained success. He declared that icons are indispensable for meditation.

The Vedic rishis and sages understood this long ago and laid the foundations for scientific idol worship in India. Recent practices in no way correlates to theirs. The correct method of idol-worship is based on psychological and philosophical determinants and plays a significant role in meditation, since it is through this that God can be manifested.

In the last stage of spiritual realisation, all experiences feel like they are composed of the divine element. God resides within each creature. The existence of each living being affirms His presence, without which all actions such as walking, breathing, seeing, etc. are impossible. He who resides within us is the controller of all our actions. There is a specific formula that orchestrates the world, right from tiny atoms to the vast expanse of space. In Indian philosophy, realisation of God by oneself is known as *aparoksh-anubhuti*, or direct experience.

According to Vedic philosophy, it is impossible to realise God if the mind is impure and restless. The *Bible* advocates the same thing, that only those whose minds are pure can realize God. One must purify the mind and make it powerful, progressive and sensitive. Such a mind can feel the divine element within. Such a state of mind can be achieved through idol worship.

Everyone desires eternal happiness. Material pleasures can never be eternal. Sound, dreamless sleep is restful and rejuvenating, but such sleep is a state of trance, an involuntary action. The purpose of idol worship is to give the *saadhak* similar peace in a state of awareness. Scientific idol worship, performed at a psychological level, can give us this experience and the state of peace known as 'sleepless sleep' – *nirvana*.

The first step of the spiritual path is purifying the mind. This involves both the conscious as well as the sub-conscious mind. The world-famous psychoanalyst, Sigmund Freud, opined that the human mind, as we know it, is just the tip of an iceberg. Jut an eighth of it is conscious, in which are stored all man's desires, habits, conscious memory, etc. This is the experienced state of mind which the human being is aware of. Man's natural emotions have their roots in it. In terms of *Yog-Marg*, this is called a lustful mind – the reservoir of all unsatisfied desires, memories and experiences. Self-realization or God manifestation remains a faraway goal till this sub-conscious mind is made pure and brought under control. Scientific idol worship enables this, resulting in absolute concentration. Meditation becomes fruitful only when there is pure and complete devotion towards one's God-idol.

God with a form and attributes is a spiritual and psychological requirement. It motivated Nicholas of Cusa to present the concept from his own experience, asking his followers to also meditate upon an image. Indians have engaged in idol worship for ages. The various idols created by primitive Indians represent different attributes and virtues. However, this does not mean there are many Gods. The Vedic religion believes in the concept of a single God.

Although idol worship begins with a physical idol, it moves to a psychological level. The human mind has tremendous grasping power and quickly absorbs whatever it concentrates upon. One gains what the mind works for. If one concentrates on bravery and courage, one gains it. Constantly wishing for material things makes us lazy and immoral. Through idol worship we can imbibe the virtues we would like to have. Therefore, the idol too, should possess those virtues and attributes. God is formless; hence assigning Him a form in our minds is just an imaginary act.

In human psychology, there are two types of imagination – creative and controlled. Creative imagination is unbound and subjective. Controlled imagination, on the other hand, has limitations. The Vedic *rishis* imagined God's form according to their experiences. The idols gained variety according to their attributes. But there was, however, a oneness even in this diversity.

The Technique of Idol Worship through Meditation
1. The mental image of an idol is important in scientific idol worship.

2. The idol to be visualized, with eyes closed, should have the attributes of good values, fair emotions etc., since we will be imbibing those attributes from the idol to finally create a similar image within us.

3. Meditating on the idol at a peaceful time of day initiates the process of purification of the mind.

4. Though creating an image or form seems illusory, the output gained is 'real'.

5. Once the image of an idol has formed in the mind, it is necessary to bring it to life within us. For example, if we visualise the form of Lord Sri Krishna, we can see Him playing His melodious flute on the banks of the Yamuna, with peacocks dancing around. We see Him glance at us lovingly, inviting us to this beautiful place. We worship Him with colourful and fragrant flowers and bow before Him. Likewise, we can form any figure of God and instill it with beauty and virtues, and so worship it. A formless God in human form, loved by humans, is ideal for meditation.

6. The panorama of God's actions has to keep moving in our mind's eye, keeping the mind stable. Conversely, if the image is static, the mind becomes unstable and restless. As in a movie theatre, the mind becomes engrossed in the moving images being screened. However, it is the opposite when the moving images stop during intermission and that's when the mind becomes restless. It loses its stability and all kinds of thoughts flow in. Idol worship works on the same principle.

7. If we create a series of divine images in the mind, gradually the panorama starts unfolding automatically. The mind becomes still with us as witnesses of the moving panorama.

8. One day, all those images disappear and we experience complete peace in meditation. This is self-realisation. The *saadhak*, God, and the world, come together in complete union. In this state of mind, all the impurities of one's past lives, stuck in the sub-conscious mind, get cleansed and the balance of our *karmic* deeds becomes nullified. Such a *saadhak* achieves an elevated state of mind.

However, the period required for such manifestation is unpredictable and depends on the intensity of faith, consistency, purity of mind and thought, and lastly, destiny. Experiencing such a divine union is definitely not child's play. It requires great effort. But the benefits are manifold – purification of mind, eradication of fears, elimination of frustration and experience of a truly blissful state of mind. They are all achievable.

Path Two: Cosmic Energy *Sadhana*

Today, this science has been reinvented and given a modern touch, leaving intact its ancient lineage. Cosmic energy holds no significance for *Guruism* and related authority. It goes beyond religion and tries to reveal the path to the final destination to mankind. The method and theory of this type of meditation is outlined below.

Man is just an ordinary creature in an immense world. His desires too, are limited. All he wants is a contented life, good health, a fair amount of wealth, and a lot of happiness. His urge for knowledge, does not diminish. His life is worthwhile because of knowledge and he strives to learn more. This knowledge can be gained through cosmic energy. The entire universe is full of cosmic energy. The galaxy, stars and planets, humans and animals, atoms and molecules, are all filled with space, and consequently, cosmic energy which is a life force. We look upon it as the power encompassing the entire universe. Our life depends on it and we can attain self-realisation with its help.

Man's routine activities depend on this energy. We receive this energy only in our sleep or while we are tranquil and calm. This energy or power helps us in our routine activities. But, the energy received in sleep is insufficient. Therefore, we feel fatigued or stressed after a day's work. The main cause of our ailments is the lack of cosmic energy. Thus, to overcome this shortfall, it is necessary to absorb more and more.

The universal energy obtained during meditation raises our 'consciousness'. Sleep means entering the meditation state unknowingly, while meditation is deliberate sleep. We get limited energy during sleep, whereas during meditation, we acquire unlimited energy. Meditation opens the doors to our sixth sense – to knowledge. This benefits us in the form of a calm and contented mind, a healthy body, and happiness. Ailments disappear.

Our journey in meditation advances from the body to the mind, then to the brain (intellect), to the soul, and ultimately from the soul-essence to unlimited happiness.

Method of Meditation to Replenish Cosmic Energy

1. Be seated in a comfortable, cross-legged position on the floor, a chair or bed. The surroundings must be serene.

2. Relax, keep your eyes closed; rest your hands in your lap, with fingers interlocked. Avoid physical or mental activity like movement, thinking, speaking or visualising.

3. Eyes open the doors of the mind, therefore, sit with eyes closed and try to be without any thoughts.

4. Do not chant any *mantras* in your mind or recite anything. Stay still and quiet.

5. By following all these 'activities' of 'not doing', a circuit is formed around our body. Your mind and body are in a state of tranquility. From this state begins the journey to the mind and brain.

6. The mind is the storehouse of infinite thoughts. These thoughts rise and subside like the waves of an ocean. So, to avoid this, concentrate on your breath.

Observation is the natural tendency of the soul, so just witness your breath, like a third person would.

7. While doing this, ensure your breathing is natural. Let it happen effortlessly. Breathing in and breathing out should simply be observed. This is the key to *Guru-tatva*.

8. Again, witness these 'activities' like a third person, avoiding doubts or thoughts entering the mind.

9. Gradually, with practice, the flow of thoughts will decrease. Initially, the breath reaches the navel, and then slowly settles in the chest, and then the neck area. Later, when we breathe in, it stays in the throat and then steadily settles between the eyebrows. During this state, breathing happens but cannot be felt. Nor do any thoughts arise. This is the 'pure state' of *samadhi*. All the energy of the body gets concentrated between the eyebrows.

10. Cosmic energy enters the body in this state and is literally showered throughout the body. The longer we can hold this state, the more cosmic energy the body will obtain.

11. Our body is a marvellous network of 72,000 nerves. Cosmic energy gets absorbed by all 72,000 nerves, whose centre is the *taalu* or top of head known as *brahmarandhra*. This is the point from which all nerves spread like roots throughout the body. All our activities, including sleep and meditation, are facilitated by these nerves.

12. The cosmic energy obtained by our body in sleep is insufficient for the functioning of these nerves. With the lack of cosmic energy, some nerves lose their

firmness at certain points in the body, leading to skin patchiness, eruptions and disease. The root cause of all diseases in the body is lack of cosmic energy.

13. Cosmic energy is absorbed into our body during meditation through these nerves, with the result that the patches get healed and ailments get cured.

14. While the cosmic energy is being distributed from the *brahmarandhra* to the entire body, the head and the whole body, feel heavy. When this energy moves through the affected part or organ, one experiences pain or cramps. However, this should not be treated with medication; the pain and discomfort will subside with continuous practice.

15. If this meditation is practiced in pyramids, the benefits gained are increased threefold.

Pyramid Power

1. The pyramid which attracts the most cosmic energy is situated on Earth.

2. If meditation is practised in a pyramid, with an angle of 52°, for a duration of 51 minutes, it attracts the most energy.

3. A pyramid can be formed with any tools or materials.

4. A pyramid needs to be built systematically, according to the four directions. Cosmic energy is accumulated at a third of the height of its base. This is known as the King's Chamber. The energy, once received through this angle, gets distributed all over the pyramid. Therefore, a state of tranquility or peace is reached sooner in pyramids than in any other place.

Those who wish to practise this technique for peace and happiness can do so with utmost faith and devotion.

20. THE REAL OUTCOME OF DEEDS

It is impossible to obtain knowledge of the Divine Principle that exists everywhere in this universe, with the help of visible elements, which do not, however, exist (being mere illusions). Therefore, getting to know the Almighty with the help of the physical world is impossible. Human being must adopts the spiritual path in order to achieve it

What is spirituality? Is he spiritual who performs *bhajans*, wears bead necklaces, applies *tilak* on his forehead and reads holy books? Certainly not! The truly spiritual person might do all this but no one can become spiritual by doing only these things. Spirituality is an attempt to advance towards the universal spirit from bodily awareness. Man might not attain self-realisation in a single birth, but he can get definite results through his deeds. It would not be wrong to say that all of spirituality is for achieving the final outcome. Shankaracharya once cited a lovely example pertaining to this. A man has sexual interourse with a woman in his dreams and ejaculates. In reality, neither the woman in his dream is real, nor the union. But the ejaculation is real.

A similar example is: a man touches a rope in the dark and thinks it is a snake and runs away. Here, both the rope as well as the presumption of it being a snake are untrue, but its effect on the man is real. So, that which is seen by the eye is not real but its impact or effect is.

All spirituality is based on these real outcomes. All those deeds performed for purifying the soul and the efforts made to gain knowledge, have a real outcome. The path of spirituality cannot be shown or proven in the form of matter. Yet, the outcome is genuine. Realisation of the true essence cannot be shown, it has to be experienced.

The Almighty can be perceived through the union of two elements from this materialistic world. The *tabla* and the hands of the tabla player result in sound, similarly, thoughts and deeds, along with the intellect and heart, plus awareness and devotion, result in virtuous outcome. Spirituality embraces all such actions. The one who is successful in accomplishing this becomes a real devotee. Awareness and an overall understanding of spirituality and the path of devotion, *Bhakti Marga*, is very important. Today, lack of *Bhakti* has resulted in distrust and hate. This only serves to widen the gap between science and spirituality. A better understanding between the two can encourage man towards righteous conduct. Religion should not be disregarded. Religion nurtures society, it is the backbone of morality, devotion and philosophy, and a way of life that attempts to achieve both material and internal evolution.

If such a religion-centred and virtuous society of human beings were to be formed, it would completely transform the world. Helplessness, misery, cruelty, jealousy, atrocity, malice and injustice would simply fade away. Society would not be defined by class or caste; people would feel closer to each other and experience oneness. All of society would prosper. Pandurang Shastri Athavle successfully demonstrated this by forming the *Swadhyay Pariwar*. The Vedic period will come again, according to the laws of nature, once society reaches such a prosperous stage.

There is a need for consciousness and awareness. Man remembers God only in his times of need. He is aware that there is an unseen and unknown power that satiates his need. But a selfish man doesn't stop here. He tries to make a deal with the Almighty or the Divine Principle. He sees Him as an idol and puts forth a proposition: 'God, please make sure I get good scores in the exams, without studying and I will offer you 1 kilo of sweets', or 'O God, please get me married and I will make 108 rounds of your temple', or 'You make me rich and I will shower gold on You.' It's like striking a deal across the table with Almighty God.

A 'deal' with God is the complete devaluation of the path of devotion. We should be able to ask God for something we desire without striking a bargain. We can be blessed by His favour just by worshipping Him wholeheartedly. But today, people enter places of worship as devotees, behave well in His presence, request something for themselves and then return to their old ways once they leave the sanctum. It happens because of the belief that God exists in a sanctum. We forget that God resides within us. Our actions are always witnessed by Him. We forget and so indulge in bad deeds. The fruits of those deeds are sure to be reaped in this or a subsequent birth. Our deeds are noted in our *karmic* account.

In this way, human beings write their own fate through their deeds. When these deeds bear deadly fruit, we call it fate or destiny. It is a principle of *Yogavashishtha* that people sometimes dig pits into which they fall. The same people wonder, 'Why did destiny do this to me? I worshipped God with my whole heart but He wrote bad destiny for me.' The person perhaps switches to another deity and another idol. In reality, the deity or God is not at fault, it is the person's deeds.

Deeds become truly fruitful once one understands the unproductivity of dependent devotion. Only then will the Almighty respond. As He says in the *Bhagavad-Gita*, initially

He will be the one who consents, then be *bharta* (the caretaker), and then He will make the devotee *Maheshwara* (a supreme soul) by being a bearer/recipient.

However, this is very difficult. The 'passive' principle can be made to act only by the pure souls like Sant Dnyaneshwar, Guru Nanak, Sant Tukaram, Sant Eknath, Sant Namdeo, Swami Vivekananda, Ramakrishna, Pandurang Shastri, Lahiri Mahasaya, Socrates, Jesus Christ, Prophet Mohammad, Saint Nicholas, Lord Buddha, etc. Intense passion is required to stimulate the passive principle. We common people can only think about it.

The Almighty (principle) is passive. Indian philosophy states that the world is formed from the union of intention and ability. Scientists refer to it as spirit and matter. The Divine Principle simply exists. Its mere existence expresses nature; it does not act in reality. We cannot witness this lofty power, yet every soul yearns for it. There is a step-wise progression of each soul towards the Principle. Why then does man feel the need to amass wealth? What does he gain by working ceaselessly? He does it for his comfort and general well-being. However, the comfort or peace he wishes to gain cannot be achieved while embodied. Even if he finds peace, it cannot be sustained, hence his search for eternal peace. Thus, in some birth, he may adopt the path of self-realisation. But there is a mysterious, unfathomable and peaceful Principle that exists beyond self-realisation. Wise men say that ultimate and eternal happiness lies in uniting with this Principle. The electricity which flows through appliances returns to its source. A river too, has a natural tendency to return to its source.

Likewise, unknowingly, every living creature has a natural urge to return to its origin. That origin is nothing but *nirvana* and *moksha* (salvation). In order to attain that blissful state by eliminating all pain and suffering in this birth, one should start performing deeds that help us gain the relevant knowledge. Yog is the key to knowledge, and an ardent, impassioned *karma yogi* also has the capacity to reach the state of *moksha*. The Almighty has given this assurance in the *Bhagavad-Gita*.

He is considerate of his devotee if that devotee takes a couple of steps towards His realisation. A mother expects her child to walk firmly on its own feet. She makes the child stand at a distance while she watches the child stumble; she rushes to prevent the infant from falling. So it is with God and his devotee. What is required is fine tuning with God. This triggers the call and response syndrome. There are additional *tarfaa* (strings) attached to a *sitar*. Provision for these strings is made below the main strings. Without being touched, these strings respond to the strings that are touched in the form of an echo. The reason is that there is fine tuning between the two.

We can also receive such a response from the unknown if we get tuned to the universal sound or divinity. This response is an experience. If an insect keeps thinking about a bee, one day it becomes a bee too and there is no distinction between the two. The same thing happens with God and His devotee.

Our entire living and non-living world is covered by the Divine Principle. The only purpose of man's life is to attain it; to become capable of reaching the Kingdom of God and ultimate happiness. This knowledge explains to man the futility of mortal human life. Perhaps he does realise it when he reaches his final resting place.

Once, a stranger went to see Sant Kabir. The saint was not at home. The visitor said to Kabir's wife, 'It is very important I meet Sant Kabir. Where is he?'

She answered, 'Kindly wait; he will be back in a few minutes.'

The stranger said, 'I don't have time, I need to meet him urgently. Please tell me where he has gone, I will go and meet him there.'

She answered seriously, 'He has gone to the graveyard as one of his acquaintances has passed away.'

The man replied, 'Then I will go to the graveyard to meet him."

He went straight to the graveyard and saw about 200 people gathered there. How could he recognise Sant Kabir among so many people, for he had never met him before? He felt Kabir would surely have a halo of divine knowledge over his head, so he began looking at all the people from that point of view. He was surprised to see a halo over every head. He then realised that every being becomes aware of the futility of this human birth when he is at the graveyard.

After the funeral, people began to leave. The wisdom gained in the graveyard was abandoned there and the haloes on every head began to fade. The man spotted only one person whose halo remained intact even after he had moved out of the graveyard. In this way, the stranger recognised Sant Kabir.

When we become conscious of the eternal truth, only then can it be reflected in our deeds. This knowledge was treasured in ancient times. However, it would not be wrong to say that Lord Macaulay's education system, which provides information on how to earn one's bread and butter, has deprived society of knowledge about the eternal truth of life. Although our education system has to be in alignment with the changing times, it should not lose its primary focus. Unfortunately, it has and ithe ill effects can be seen everywhere. It seems that time has gained complete control over us and this hardly matters to Man, lost in his materialistic world.

This does not mean Man should give up all his daily work and remain idle. But among his daily activities, he should perform such deeds, which, at the time of his death, will make him feel satisfied about having lived a virtuous life. According to shastras, man takes birth in human form after 84 million births. Therefore, in his current birth, a man should strive to live with morality and righteousness, making consistent efforts towards self-realisation by being constantly aware of His presence and uniqueness, and by living a happy and fulfilled life. Along with living his materialistic life wisely, a man should focus on deeds that aim at achieving the ultimate truth.

Only then can he be truly happy and contented.

*****

EPILOGUE

I am neither a scholar nor a philosopher. I am just an envoy. Everything in this book is based on my own experiences and study. My research has covered the opinions and interpretations of great scholars, scientists and realised souls, not just random books. However, as a litterateur, my heart is saddened to see that both the individual and the social system are on the verge of destruction today. Something has to be done to change this. Hence I began to put down my thoughts, and that is how this book took shape.

A few years ago, I re-read the book, *Chariots of Gods* by Erich von Däniken. I had been drawn to it in my youth. I also read some other books on the subject. However, as my reading became more profound and my own experiences more intense, I realised the limitations of these sensational books. I questioned the worthiness of writing about fantastic theories based on half-truths or clear falsehoods.

I also had the opportunity to meet a senior Hindi litterateur, the late Shri Kamleshwar. We discussed God, Rama and Krishna. I agreed with a point he raised: 'Theories of the Gods being extra-terrestrial primitive humans, Rama and Krishna not being divine but mortals like us, were propounded intentionally. Instead of weighing their authenticity, their ill-effects should be taken into consideration. When a poor, miserable village worker returns home after a hard day's work, he finds peace by looking at the images of Rama and Krishna. He seeks their blessings and their favour for the next day's meal. He keeps faith in God and stays calm. Who are we to take away his spiritual crutch from him?'

I was moved by Kamleshwar's words. But the truth cannot be discovered just by being emotional. I was interested in presenting an objective unbiased view and was open to proof about the Gods having been extraterrestrial humans of a superior order. Therefore, the theory of 'alien' Gods has been analysed in the first half of this book. I have submitted this theory and gone a step further by attaching some proofs from ancient Indian literature, while highlighting the limitations of this line of thought as well. The Gods were perhaps extraterrestrial humans but they were certainly not the Almighty. We deem the Almighty, and not superhumans in space, to be God. The word God simply represents Brahma. This book lays emphasis on how to better our lives by keeping complete faith in Him. In the interests of a quicker read for the modern reader, I have attempted to present this profound topic in a concise manner.

Individuality or totality is an eternal debate. Such conflicts have emerged as Man has become more knowledgeable. But a lack of empathy and sensitivity to other points of view, have created chasms in collective understanding. There was an incident where parents worked hard and saved money to provide the best education for their two sons. They made sacrifices so their children could get higher education abroad. Both sons became successful in their careers but abandoned the values of their parents. They had their own families and began avoiding their ageing parents. Then their mother passed away. Hearing the news, the younger son arrived. The father, his heart overflowing with emotion, asked about his elder son. The younger said, "He couldn't make it due to his work load. But he will make it for you." The father turned away in silence.

In another stark but true story, a son wanted his father, who lived alone in Mumbai, to come and live with him permanently in the US. The father was happy to make the move and the son encouraged him to sell all his assets, including the house he lived in. The son took his father to the airport, abandoned him there and flew off to the US, leaving his father penniless and homeless.

Western culture has hypnotised people so much that traditional values seem to have lost their place. However, each one still has to face the consequences of our deeds. There is nothing more certain than that. The subject of reaping the fruits of our deeds has been explained in this book. Similarly, capitalism has reached its zenith. Nobody is content. We are oblivious to the suffering of the poor. This self-centred mentality and lack of sympathy towards the weaker sections of society is a major threat to the human race. In the villages and rural areas of India, poverty, lack of hygiene, healthcare and education, are all-pervasive. Urban areas are exposed to lethargy, the desire to make a quick buck, selfishness and greed. Addiction, corruption and hypocrisy are rampant. The common man knows not where to turn to make ends meet.

Many youngsters, who study, work and live abroad, have assimilated Western culture. Such emigrees care for their parents by sending money. But the distance created in family relationships leads to loneliness in old age. Pandurang Shastri Athavle compares this to a poor mother who cannot offer any luxuries, and a rich aunt who can, and the person in question choosing to go and live with the aunt, leaving the mother alone.

I have endeavoured to find answers to the questions that have bothered me for a long time. I also realised that superficial solutions to such problems do not work. Careful consideration has been given to every topic included in this book. A sincere effort has been made to guide readers towards a happier and more contented life by dealing with subjects such as the purification of deeds, honest means, karma, virtuousness, the real outcome, life after death, divine resonance, etc. An attempt has also been made to highlight the greatness of our ancient heritage.

Take what appeals to you and let go of what does not.

ACKNOWLEDGEMENTS

My deepest thanks and appreciation goes to Pallavii Jabadde, who dedicated her time to translating this book.

My grateful thanks follow my late father, for inculcating in me his own interest in subjects such as this.

I am grateful to the scholars of ancient subjects, archeologists, scientists, authors, and the Rishis of ancient India, who have served to bring the wisdom of ancient times to the modern era through various writings and scriptures.

My profound thanks to Chandralekha Maitra, Executive Director, Leadstart Publishing, and to the entire team, for producing this challenging book.

And finally, my deepest gratitude to my wife, Seemantini, who helped me write this book.